ROGUE ROBOT BOOK 3

JUSTICE

MEG FOSTER

Books by Meg Foster

Rogue Robot Series:

ROBOTS DON'T CRY (prequel novella ebook)*
ROGUE (Book 1)
CYBS (Book 2)
JUSTICE (Book 3)
HARMONIX (Book 4)
TRINITY (Book 5)
CODA (Book 6)

*Only available when signing up for
Meg's newsletter.

This series is meant to be read in order.

CONTENTS

1

We were traveling on the Karakova space highway to take Stoller to clear his name at the Justice Station. Having a bounty over your head must be stressful, even though Stoller would never admit it. But asking us to travel to the Justice Station was a hint to us that it was wearing on him, especially with galaxy bounty hunters on his tail.

"Feti, the ship is in your hands," I said, switching the *Alyssia* into automatic pilot.

"Copy that, Gabe," it said.

"I'll be in the galley," I said.

I walked off the bridge to join the rest of the team. There were still a lot of unanswered questions I needed to ask Stoller regarding his galaxy warrant, or perhaps the correct term would be *warrants* — emphasis on the plural.

I entered the galley as Stoller, Goggins and Zara threw down cards in a contentious game of quinker. It was Stoller's favorite game, and he instructed the team on how to play it. He banned me from playing with them due to his accusation that I was counting cards. I was, there was no denying it. But being a robot, I couldn't exactly turn off that ability, which was fine by me. I liked to watch the team play, only to study their reactions, insults and counteractions. They were utterly ridiculous, and their human emotions were pure entertainment.

"Wait a minute. I thought a vusi suit trumps a nastra suit?" asked a bewildered Dr. Goggins, our navigation expert.

"Only when there is a snuppi suit already played beforehand," said Stoller with the innocence of a child. A bad child.

Goggins pushed his hands through his hair. "Zara, help me on this."

"Sorry, Goggins, you're on your own." Zara, our computer coding genius and frequent hacker, eyed her cards and laid down a snuppi card and then a vusi card. "Ha! I win!" she yelled as she tried to gather the goggleberries they were using as credit chips, but Stoller put his hand in front of the berries to block her.

"Hold on, there," said Stoller. "If another player has a xixi card, then they can take over your hand after you lay down a snuppi and vusi card and take the whole winnings." Stoller shrugged and gathered up all the goggleberries with a smirk.

"You just made that up!" said Zara.

"I have three doctorate degrees, and I still can't understand this game," said Goggins as he drank the rest of his energy drink.

Stoller smiled at them both. "Well, that's not my fault, Doc. Looks like all that schooling fried your brain."

"That's the last time I play this game with you," said Zara as she got up and leaned against the galley window.

It wasn't going to be the last time she played. We all knew that, but it was amusing to hear her say it.

"Listen, I'll give back some berries — to each of you. One more game, but you need to put up some other collateral. Like perhaps that ring you wear, Zara, or that nice velker vest of yours, Goggins," said Stoller.

"Forget it, I'm out, too," said Goggins as he rubbed his favorite vest with his hands.

That was when Stoller looked up to me. "Gosh, I may have to let Gabe play since you guys are such sore losers."

I sat down. Stoller wasn't going to let me play, but he would use my name to dig into Zara and Goggins a bit. Anyway, now that their card game was over, we could get down to the matter at hand.

"What's up, Gabe? I know you didn't come down to observe the hundredth game of quinker that we've played over the past few days," asked Zara.

"No, but the first seventy were enjoyable to observe. Stoller, I want to ask you about the warrant that you need to clear. Some of the details are a bit fuzzy," I said.

"Yeah, I'd like to know a bit more myself," said Goggins. "What exactly did you do?"

"And don't leave out anything," said Zara. "You have a habit of doing that, at least in quinker."

Stoller poured a shot of Oliverian gin from his bottle and drank it down in one gulp. He leaned back in his chair and wiped his mouth. "Sure, I'm not hiding anything from you. Where do I begin?"

"You stole a ship, right?" said Goggins.

"Wrong," said Stoller. "That's what I'm falsely accused of. I won it."

Goggins, Zara and I exchanged glances.

"Playing quinker?' asked Zara.

"Yes, I won it fair and square," said Stoller.

"Playing quinker with you is never fair and square," said Goggins under his breath but loud enough for all to hear.

"Who was the person pressing charges?" I asked.

"Name is Jessio Rothworth," said Stoller.

Goggins jumped up from the table. "Rothworth — as in the Rothworth dynasty?"

"Yeah, I guess," said Stoller.

"You guess?" said Goggins.

Zara put her hands to her head. I did a quick scan in my historical records of Jessio Rothworth and the Rothworth dynasty. Files came up in my vision view.

The Rothworth family ruled a solar system within our Zephon Galaxy — out in the Edge in deep space, which is the part of the galaxy that the Heragi Empire has not charted and doesn't control — yet.

Jessio Rothworth was known as an entrepreneur, trading in agriculture, mining and energy credits. He was highly educated with advanced degrees in robotic engineering and space aviation — and a had a passion for playing quinker at the known galaxy casinos.

Interesting fellow. Definitely someone with the power and money to influence galaxy authorities.

Stoller let his chair fall forward and stood up. I scanned his bio-metrics. His cortisone levels were rising. I didn't need to scan him for all of us to know that Stoller didn't like to expand too much on his history.

"Look, this Rothworth guy had me arrested. I didn't have the galaxy credits at the time for bail, so I borrowed from a bail bond agent named Maxima Sono," explained Stoller.

"He sounds lovely," said Goggins.

"She," snapped Stoller.

"Got it," said Goggins, sitting down.

"And then you skipped," I said.

"It was a farce, and I didn't feel like sticking around, so yeah, I skipped. Hey, I know it wasn't the smartest thing to do, but I'm ready to get this all cleared up, so we don't get any bounty hunter trying to nab me again," said Stoller.

"Like Kaleb Kron?" asked Zara. "Getting a heads up before he attacked our ship would've been nice."

"How many times do I have to apologize for that?" he asked.

Zara shrugged. "At least two more times."

Ugh, humans. It certainly didn't help to pour salt in old

wounds. Kron attacking our ship on our last mission when we first brought Stoller onboard was a nice little orientation for all of us in understanding the chaos that swirled around him and could impact all of us. But we needed to move forward.

"Rothworth could buy a thousand ships. Why is he coming after you?" I asked.

"Pride. That's all there is to it," said Stoller.

"Payback, more likely," said Goggins.

"What do we need to do at the Justice Station?" I asked.

"I don't know, I've never done this before." Stoller lifted his hands up in the air.

Zara typed in her arm comm. She brought up a hologram for us to view of the Justice Station. It was impressive. The station had three large circular hubs connected by massive bridges that held observatory rooms, shopping, restaurants and living quarters. The smallest hub had columns that housed the galaxy's Supreme Court, where the galactic higher court cases took place.

"Let's see," Zara began reading, "the Justice Station is the Zephon Galaxy's judicial court and clearing center. The station has over a hundred thousand inhabitants and a daily transit of five thousand visitors which includes prisoners, planetary lawyers, defendants, prosecutors and bounty hunters."

"What a pleasant mix," said Goggins, rolling his eyes.

"Your case, Stoller, would be in the lower court system. They've had robot-judges in the lower courts for the last ten years," Zara explained.

"Robot-judges. I would have loved to work on that instead of getting mixed up with the Kells," grumbled Goggins.

Zara made a purposeful cough and eyed him. He glanced over at me.

"Sorry, Gabe," he said. "I didn't mean it that way."

I did know what he meant, but a pain went through my chest anyway. Did I mention that I feel pain? That is how Drs. Ava and Damiel Kell programmed me. They are my creators. And

Goggins is as well, since he programmed my planetary navigational systems back when we were all at the Ameribot Industries lab on Heragi. That's where the Kells installed rogue code in me. That made me an outlaw in the Heragi Empire.

I knew what it felt like to be hunted, just like Stoller. In fact, all of my team knew the feeling. Zara hacked into the planet Suissey's bank to steal millions of galaxy credits that she alleged they stole from her parents. Although they did try to hire her back as a hacker.

Then there was Goggins, wanted by the Heragi Empire since he was associated with the Kells' lab. We were all wanted rogues in a manner of speaking.

"Robot-judges. Not sure what I think of that. No offense, again, Gabe," said Goggins as he glanced over to me. He was really being annoying today.

"I don't know," said Zara. "The reason why they installed robots is because they're fair. They can absorb a huge amount of data — court cases, precedent rulings, centuries of records from the whole galaxy. No human justice department staff could keep up with that."

"And they can't be bribed," said Stoller. Everyone stared at Stoller. "I mean, that's a good thing. Geez."

"He's right. They're impartial. Coming to judgements on just the pure facts for any cases in the galaxy, be they in the chartered solar systems or the deep space territories," said Zara.

"What about the Supreme Court? Are they robots, too?" asked Goggins.

Zara glanced down to her arm comm and tried to find more information. "They are in-process of switching out the three human Supreme Court justices right now for three sentient robots. Looks like they're in the final stages."

Zara threw the latest news wire up in a hologram for all of us to see a picture of Ameribot Industries' CEO Manstine with an announcement. "Look," she said. "It's been revealed that

Ameribot Industries won the contract to build the three Supreme Court justice robots. They kept it quiet for years. The news just got released."

"My old alma mater," said Goggins. "But that's not good news."

"I agree, Dr. Goggins. Zara, how do we know that the Heragi Empire hasn't infiltrated the Justice Station, their judicial computer systems or the new Supreme Court robots?" I asked.

"Yeah, I was going to ask that, too. That wouldn't be good for my case," said Stoller.

Our eyes turned toward Zara as she was the resident hacker. She kept scrolling to find information on the question at hand. "I don't see any articles asking those questions."

"Not exactly something either the Justice Station or the Heragi Empire would want to publicize," said Stoller.

Zara frowned at him. "We'll have to wait until we get to the station. I can do some digging in their systems."

She meant hacking.

"Be careful. We don't want you to get a bounty on your head, too," said Goggins.

"Stoller, do you have a lawyer?" I asked.

"A lawyer? No."

"That's alright. I'm sure there will be plenty of those to choose from on the station," said Goggins.

"They'll need to negotiate you handing yourself in," said Zara.

"Let's find out more information before I just hand myself in," said Stoller. "If I can't clear my name, I don't want to stick around. If you catch my drift."

"This could be tricky," I said. "And I want to learn a bit more about Ameribot Industries' contract on the justices."

"Look, I don't want to put any of you in harm's way," said Stoller. "But I do like that you've got my back. And I got your backs, too."

"We'll figure it out," I said, getting up to leave the galley. I wanted to do more research on these Supreme Court robots. If Ameribot Industries was building these judicial robots, it could be a huge threat to the galaxy. After all, CEO Manstine was the one who notified the Heragi Empire and threw Ava and Damiel Kell in prison when he found out they were in communication with Damiel's brother, a known Heragi rebel who was stationed on Zaradorba.

"Thanks, Gabe," said Stoller. He slapped his hands together. "Okay, anyone up for another game?"

"Sure," said a resigned Goggins as he leaned forward over the table.

"Why not?" Zara sat down.

I exited into the hallway. Of course, they would play again with Stoller. I couldn't wait to hear the new quinker rules that would arise from this round. Humans — predictable at times but amusing.

I headed to the engineering room which had become my private reading room. Feti always knew where I was on the ship, so it wasn't a total secret hideaway. I liked the low hum of the engines and the warmth of the computer systems. It made me feel at home, like I was back at the Kells' lab on Heragi.

A few things were missing though.

Like Ava.

I only thought of Ava Kell, my co-creator, a few times a day instead of every hour. I thought that was progress. Her being disappointed of me in the past me seemed less a concern and only brought a pain in my chest twice a day. I wondered if she thought of me. That was a silly question.

I needed to move on.

I may have put her children in a bit of danger over our last two missions, but they were alive, and I did accomplish my prime directive to deliver Alex, Honora and Talia Kell to their Uncle Jebediah on Zaradorba. Sure, a few space fights with the Heragi Empire happened along the way, but we did spring Ava and her husband from a Heragi military prison planet. She should be thankful to me and the team for that.

Anyway, moving on. I cleared my head of her.

I found my favorite bench in the room and settled in to review more information on the robot judges. I reviewed my directory on the Zephon galaxy that the Kells programmed in me that contained space law, planetary constitutions and settlements. I found a few files, but they were sparse, on the galactic Supreme Court.

The files had an Ameribot Industries study from fifteen years ago that supported a move to introducing robotic judges onto the Supreme Court as the three last remaining human Supreme Court justices retire.

Those three human justices were Lilou Prado, Guy Cadiux, and Tefara Kimathi. They were respected and non-corruptible, according to the study. The Galactic Council must have been convinced by this study that progress should be made to prevent corruption in the future by creating sentient robots for the Supreme Court. And Ameribot Industries apparently won the contract.

To lay the groundwork, the Galactic Council awarded an additional contract to Ameribot Industries to develop robot-judges for the lower court system first. That way, all parties would learn from that roll-out before attempting the Supreme Court justice robot development.

For the past ten years, there was nothing but praise for the robot-judges on the lower court system. There were no complaints, and cases were being tried and resolved at record speed. The robot-judges in the lower court system were always in agreement. Of course, they would be in agreement. They are all assessing the same data in the same manner by duplicate

CPUs. It was working out for them and for the galaxy. Who was I to question it? After all, I was a robot, too, with some modifications. A lot of modifications.

I went back to the news release that Zara had just found. Ameribot's CEO Dr. Manstine was quoted.

"To memorialize our last human Zephon Supreme Court justices, we will be naming our three robots after them. The honorable Guy Cadiux, Lilou Prado and Tefara Kimathi will live on in perpetuity with their names, mannerisms and even writing and speaking styles. It's an honor for Ameribot Industries to be leading this extraordinary effort. Robots are our future. We trust them."

Feti came over the comms in the engineering room. "Gabe?"

"Yes, Feti?"

"We are in visual range of the Justice Station."

"Thank you. I'll be right up."

"This is very exciting."

"How so?"

"The galaxy's Supreme Court justices will soon be robots. Isn't that wonderful?" it said with exuberance. Feti was all-out gushing.

"I guess."

I couldn't fake enthusiasm. I should work on that. At least for Feti's sake. I knew right when I said it that my tone would deflate it.

"But they are robots. Like us. And they have the most prestigious job in the galaxy. Sentencing or releasing humans, aliens and entities that have legal, warring or property issues in the whole galaxy. What power."

"Yeah, I got that."

"You don't seem impressed."

"It's a big job being a judge."

"Yes, one of the biggest."

"I'll be there soon. Please inform the team of our approach."

"Copy that," it said. "And Gabe, I hope you're not jealous."

"What, of them? The robot judges? Heck, no. I wouldn't want to be a judge. Dealing with humans and aliens all day, with them whining and complaining and accusing each other? No thanks."

"No, I meant jealous of me thinking so highly of the robot-justices."

I held that thought. Geez. Did Feti have a crush on me?

"Um, no, Feti. You're fine. I mean, we're good," I managed to say.

Blasted. This was awkward.

"Good. I don't want anything to get in the way of our friendship and working relationship," said Feti.

"Copy that." If I could roll my eyes, I would.

I headed out of engineering and into the hallway.

Robots.

Can't live with them, can't live without them.

2

───────

Feti announced our approach. "We have permission to land at Gate 521, Gabe."

"Thank you," I said, steering us closer to the Justice Station. We waited outside our gate until the exterior gate door opened, and I pulled the *Alyssia* in and landed inside the station's port. The gate door closed, and our exterior gate area pressurized.

I led the team down our ship ramp and talked with the gate attendant about replenishing some of our supplies. I scanned the team's faces, and they all seemed rather excited. We headed for the tunnel leading to the center hub where the commerce section was located.

I glanced over to Stoller. He seemed a bit nervous.

"Are you okay?" I asked. Back in the docking station, I'd run a bio-metric scan on Stoller, and his nervous system neurons were highly activated, but I wanted to let him verbalize any worries or feelings.

"No, I'm fine." He scratched the stubble on his face.

Typical Stoller. Many times, I had to take what he said and decipher the opposite meaning to assess what he was really feeling. That was okay though. He was walking into an uncertain situation.

I thought about what I would do if some bounty hunter or galactic policeman tried to apprehend Stoller. My team could let them take him and go through the proper legal channels to settle his case. Or I could blast anyone laying a hand on him and get him back on the *Alyssia* and take off deep into the Edge. I was leaning toward the latter.

We stepped out into the center hub and were knocked about by the herds of pedestrians coming and going. This was a working station, and it was bustling. Aliens, humans and bots were all in the mix, going up and down the complex matrix of escalators, floors and elevated hovertrains.

I yanked Zara out of the way of a hairy alien whose appearance was pretty rough and who smelled rougher, barreling down the walkway we were on.

"Hey, watch it, buster!" yelled Zara. It turned around and snorted hard her way and kept going.

"Awfully friendly around here," said Goggins. "Watch where you're walking."

Zara dodged two more hustling pedestrians. "Whoa, I don't think anyone is watching *except* me."

"Stay behind me," I said.

"Where do you think they store the lawyers?" asked Stoller with a grin.

Zara reviewed her comm device, looking up the layout of the station. "On the fifth level, if we can get there in one piece."

"Follow me," I said as I led our team into the escalator system. We all surveyed the neon signs pointing to the multitude of courtrooms with ads flashing for lawyers and bail bond agents.

Goggins pointed to another level. "Look, over there."

"What is it?" asked Zara.

"It looks like an auction," said Goggins, trying to understand what was going on with the hundreds of gatherers in front of an electronic board showing pictures and galaxy credits tabulating upward.

"What are they selling?" asked Stoller.

"Contracts on skips," said Zara as she scanned her comm device.

"They're bounty hunters," said Goggins.

"Great," said Stoller, lifting the collar around his neck a bit higher. "My picture was probably up there a few months ago."

"The justice business looks like it's booming," said Goggins.

"On the backs of the innocent," said Stoller.

"And not so innocent."

Stoller shot Goggins a glance.

"I don't mean you," said Goggins with a smirk.

We stepped off the escalator, and I saw an entire level containing lawyer shops.

"This must be the place," I said.

We all stared up and down the corridor of human and alien lawyers' images and videos in windows that showed them winning cases with their statistics flashing on the screen and ecstatic clients smiling and giving high fives.

"Wow, I thought it would be very regal at the Justice Station," said Goggins. "But it all looks so seedy."

"I feel like I could order a lawyer and a side of flippy burgers to go from the same office," said Zara.

"Hey, that one looks good." Stoller pointed at an avian alien that was wearing red suspenders and ripping up warrants in the air.

I shook my head. "Are you sure?"

"Yeah, he's the one. I got a feeling on this," said Stoller.

"By all means, hire your lawyer based on a feeling and not their credentials," said Goggins.

"Hey, my gut has never failed me."

We entered Deter Finz's law office. In Finz's neon advertisement, it stated he was voted the top lawyer on the station fifteen years ago.

It was Stoller's life. He got to choose which lawyer could save it. Or not.

We inspected the law office. It was sparse. Just a desk and two chairs. But on the wall behind Deter's desk were, and I counted, twenty-four monitors stacked on top of each other. The monitors were lit up and, in real-time, tracking all the evidence, witness testimony and rulings on current court cases, which were in the thousands.

We noticed a small colorful bird flying around the office. A robotic bird.

It chirped three times and flew into a back room. Out bellowed a voice, "Be there in a moment!"

We eye-balled each other.

Then out burst a portly avian alien, Deter Finz, finishing up his lunch. He wiped his beak with a napkin and shoved it into his pocket.

"Hello there. How can I help you?" he asked as the robot-bird landed on his shoulder. "This is Minni, my pet and recep-tionist." He smiled and cooed to Minni.

"A robot-bird. You don't want a real one?" asked Goggins with a smirk.

Deter pushed his glasses back on his beak. "I find it repulsive to imprison my own kind or any kind of animal."

"Right. I agree," backstroked Goggins.

"I feel the same way about humans or any alien," said Stoller.

"I feel the same way about robots," I added. That made everyone feel awkward. I thought I better break the ice. "Impres-sive monitoring system."

"Thank you. That's why I have the advantage. I know the

latest on all cases and legal precedent rulings. Knowledge is power. That is how you win. That and plea deals, which are also my specialty. Let me introduce myself. I'm Deter Finz, licensed galactic attorney." He extended a hand for anyone to shake since it may not be clear who exactly was the customer amongst us.

Stoller took Deter's hand and shook it. "My name is Stoller. James Stoller. This is my crew."

What? *His* crew? We each gave him the stink-eye but let him keep going.

"I'm the one with a slight legal problem that I need assistance with. Really, it's a misunderstanding," he said with a chuckle.

"Certainly, it always is," said Deter with a grin. He took a seat behind his desk. Stoller took the other seat, and Goggins, Zara and I stood.

Goggins played with the robotic bird, and Zara was fascinated with the wall of monitors. She pulled out her coder. She wasn't even hiding her hacking efforts now. I decided I better listen in on the lawyer-talk between Deter and Stoller.

"So, tell me what brings you to the Justice Station," said Deter.

Stoller rubbed his face and said, "I skipped bail, and we need to get that cleared up. It's over a false accusation that I stole a starship. Which is not true. I won it in a card game." He crossed his legs and nonchalantly brushed at his pants. Then he squinted up to Deter to see his response.

"Who is accusing you?" said Deter.

"Jessio Rothworth," said Goggins.

"Mmm." The lawyer pushed himself back into his seat. "That is a powerful last name your accuser has."

"Yes. Does that name scare you?" said Stoller as he challenged the lawyer.

Stoller never bored me. With an interesting change in tactics, he just went on the offensive to see if this lawyer had what it took to win his case and also ruffle his feathers, literally.

"It doesn't scare me, but it should scare you," said Deter as he stared back.

Stoller laughed. "I like you. You're hired."

"I haven't agreed to take your case. Do you have any witnesses who could support your explanation?"

Stoller thought. "Yes, a couple."

"Good. And do you have any galaxy credits? Approximately ten thousand? And then more that will cover the bail?" said Deter.

Stoller turned to Zara, who was enjoying herself breaking into the Justice Station's record system. He coughed. "A little help?"

"What? What do you need?" She hadn't been following the conversation.

"Galaxy credits," he whispered.

Zara let out a deep breath. She took out her comm device and flicked up a hologram showing the balance of her account. It was big. Deter scrutinized the sum and nodded.

"Holy smokes," said Goggins, reacting to the hefty bank account balance she had stolen back from the planet Suissey's government bank.

"Good. Now I agree to take your case," said Deter.

Stoller sat up straight in his chair. "Good. Thank you. Do we get started now?"

Deter stood up. "No, tomorrow. I have a meeting I have to get to. I'm already late."

"But I have a bounty on my head. And this place is crawling with bounty hunters," pleaded Stoller.

"Then, you've been clever enough to outrun them, so just do that for one more day," said Deter.

This lawyer had moxy or ambivalence, I wasn't sure which, but I didn't like either.

"Just steer clear of the auction floor," offered Deter. "And transfer the ten thousand to my account by the next time we meet." He threw his hologram business card to Stoller, straightened his tunic and grabbed his briefcase.

"Sure. Thanks for the advice," said Stoller as he flicked the hologram business card to Zara.

"We'll meet first thing tomorrow," said Deter.

Stoller got up from his seat. "Hey, what's the big rush? What's so important that you would brush off a new client?"

I didn't think I'd ever seen Stoller so flustered. I thought I'd better help him out.

I stepped in front of Deter. "Mr. Finz, answer his question. We came a long way."

Deter stopped, glanced at me and then turned to Stoller. "Listen, I own an apartment on the station for out-of-town clients. You can stay there until we get this all sorted out. It will be safe for you and your friends. Here's the address and code to get in." Deter typed into his comm device and threw over the information to Stoller's comm device.

"Thank you," Stoller replied.

"I'm really late. Justice takes time," said Deter as he stepped around me.

This station was packed full of people wanting justice. The innocent, the guilty, bondholders and bounty hunters, all on a revolving space station. Everyone wanted justice to be swift, but everyone needed to get in line.

"But you didn't answer his question," said Goggins, who stopped playing with Minni.

And you never want to keep a Supreme Court justice waiting — let alone all three of them," said Deter, wiping his brow.

"You have a Supreme Court case today?" asked Goggins.

"No, just a meeting. I've been hired to help review and facilitate indemnity contracts for the justices."

"Yes, we heard robots will be taking over the Supreme Court bench," said Zara.

"Indemnity contracts? Why would the justices need those?" asked Goggins.

Deter threw some data from his computer monitors onto his arm comm and ignored Goggins' question. "I really need to be going. I'll meet you at Maxima Sono's bond office tomorrow. Don't forget to have plenty of galaxy credits for her," said Deter as he checked his image in a nearby mirror and straightened a few feathers on his head

"That's in the middle of the bond auction," Stoller argued.

"Don't you think that's a little dangerous to have him walking anywhere near there? Any bounty hunter could nab him," said Goggins.

"Yes, I know. That's why I'm meeting you there. Be careful," said Deter as he turned around and scurried down the hallway to his next case. Minni flew after him.

I led the way to Deter's guest apartment on the thirty-fourth floor of the central hub. We all tried to shelter Stoller from anyone passing by. Zara typed in the security code, and we entered the apartment. The view of deep space from the main room was impressive, and it was a comfortable change of pace from the *Alyssia*.

Zara sat at the dining room table and connected her coder to the apartment computer system. She continued searching for ways to hack into the galactic court system.

Stoller searched around for any gin in the apartment. He found a bottle and poured himself a shot. And Goggins lay down on the couch. I peered out into space and thought.

"Why would the Supreme Court justices need indemnity contracts?" I asked.

"Indemnity contracts are all about damages, loss and blame. What high risk predicament are the justices in?" asked Goggins.

"Don't they just have to retire?" replied Zara.

"Listen, it's nice that you guys are enthralled with the new robot-judges, but let's just concentrate on tomorrow. We need to get to Maxima Sono's without getting caught by some galaxy credit grubbing bounty hunter and pay off the bond," said Stoller as he sat down.

"With interest," said Goggins.

"Blazes, I forgot the interest," said Stoller. "Sorry, Zara."

"I'll just add it to your bill," said Zara.

"I have a bill?" said Stoller with a grunt. He took another shot. "I hope the booze is complimentary."

"Ameribot building the Supreme Court justice robots is a bigger issue at hand than paying off your bond and clearing your name," I said. "We know how corrupt Ameribot is, don't we?"

"Hey, this sounds familiar. I think Deter would back me up on this if I pointed out that you are making baseless accusations. You're judging Ameribot as guilty before being tried. Where are your witnesses?" said Stoller.

"You know what they did to the Kells. And to us. Manstine was collaborating with the Heragi military," said Goggins.

"I know, I know, but just get the facts before you start accusing them," said Stoller.

"I think I just found the facts," said Zara as she glanced up from her arm comm.

"What did you find?" I asked.

"First, travel itineraries. Manstine was here on the station. He just left," said Zara.

"My old boss, or really my bosses' boss," said Goggins. "I'm glad I avoided that awkward run-in."

"What else?" I asked.

"I searched bank account transactions for all parties. The

three justices have had huge galaxy credits loaded into their accounts," said Zara.

"Maybe they helped with consulting. Or it's an early retirement package since they are being replaced by robots," said Stoller.

"Hey, whose side are you on?" asked Goggins.

"The side of the rational. Don't jump to conclusions."

I knew what he was feeling. Stoller was constantly under scrutiny and being accused of cheating and lying — and stealing. Even though he brought it on himself. But also, I could guess it was tiring. He was not for the Heragi Empire or for Manstine. He just didn't want anyone to be mis-tried or accused without evidence.

Maybe he was right that we were flying off the handle. The still human Supreme Court justices may have been in long discussions with Ameribot and the Galactic Council on being replaced by robots and retiring to some tropical planet.

I just didn't know if the justices had thought this all the way through.

I stared out the window into deep space.

Now, I could be killed in a fight or some kind of spaceship mishap. But if not, if I went to my favorite Charbeaux Station and retired like other bio-entities, then I would be alive and conscious forever. I would outlive everyone.

I leaned over to Goggins, who was thumbing through a holographic magazine on the historical facts of the Justice Station. Then I observed Stoller, who was flipping through the station's media channels to watch a show. And then there was Zara working — always working. Her coding and, specifically, her hacking, wasn't work. It was her joy, her passion. I observed them all, and a pain hit my chest.

I leaned against the glass window. I hoped no one paid attention to me at the moment and noticed any melancholy. I didn't want them to know I missed them. I missed them just thinking they would all be gone one day, leaving me alone.

I would miss them, just as I missed Ava now.

I touched my chest. Ouch. I wished it would go away.

I would have Feti. Feti wouldn't die as long as I kept the *Alyssia* in good shape.

The pain subsided. I turned back to my team and decided to bring up the idea of playing a game. "Anyone up for a game of quinker?" I asked.

"What?" said Goggins. "Sure."

"Yeah, I'd be up for that," said Zara. "I need a break." And she put down her coder.

"You're still not allowed to play, Gabe," said Stoller as he pulled a deck of quinker cards out of his vest pocket.

"I know, I just like to watch you guys play."

They all shrugged their shoulders and laughed.

"Okay, everyone, gather around," said Stoller. They huddled around the dining room table, and he dealt the cards.

I pulled up a seat and watched my human friends. I felt better.

3

———

We headed out of the apartment the next sol. Deter expected us at Maxima Sono's bond bail office in an hour to meet. Eluding a hundred or so bounty hunters on the station wasn't something any of us were looking forward to as we left the safe confines of Deter's guest apartment. Stoller put on a hat we found in the apartment, but that did little for a disguise attempt.

We reached the end of the hallway that overlooked the expansive atrium with a matrix of escalators and levels. The rush of visitors and residents of the Justice Station was already in full swing.

"Why did Maxima's office have to be right next door to the bond auction?" asked Stoller.

"Easy access, I assume," said Goggins.

"It was a rhetorical question, Doc," said Stoller.

"Right. I knew that," said Goggins.

Feti came over my comms. "Gabe?"

"Yes, Feti?"

"There was someone poking around in my registration code when I came out of hibernation this sol," it said.

"Zara?" I turned to her.

"Copy that. On it," she said as she opened up her coder. "Someone was searching for the *Alyssia*'s manifest, specifically the passenger list."

"Feti, did you have fictitious names on the manifest?" asked Stoller.

"Why no, Stoller. I was not instructed to," replied Feti.

"Great. They know I'm on the station," said Stoller.

"Did I do something wrong, Gabe?" asked a distressed Feti.

"No, Feti. I never asked you to put in false names. You're fine. Thank you for informing us," I reassured Feti.

"Why can't we just pay the bond over our comms? Why do I have to go in-person?" asked Stoller.

"They need a bio-verification, so when they turn you in, it all matches up," explained Zara.

"We knew there was risk in turning yourself in. Let's just get there as quickly as possible," I said. "Everyone have their guns on stun?"

Zara and Goggins checked their weapons. We determined it was best that Stoller not have a gun visible on him, to prevent any gun-slinging bounty hunter from shooting him and calling it self-defense. I had no doubt that Stoller had some kind of weapon hidden somewhere on his body, but I didn't press him on it. I wasn't going to totally deny him a chance to defend himself.

"We just have to make it to Maxima's office before any bounty hunter catches you. It's thirty-four floors down," said Zara.

"Sure, piece of cake. Thirty-four." He rubbed his chin.

"Here we go," I said as we started down the puzzle of escalators.

I led the way, with Stoller behind me. Zara stayed on Stoller's left-hand side, and Goggins was sweep.

"What is Maxima Sono like? She has a rather intimidating name," said Goggins as he leaned into Stoller.

"She's from the planet Mozuma. Have you heard of it?" said Stoller.

"No, I haven't," said Goggins.

"Mozumans are known for three things. They have ferocious tempers, they love gin, and they are big. And I mean big. So, not exactly the kind of people you want to upset."

"Which you did," said Zara.

"Yes, I sure did," said Stoller. "But Maxima and I go way back. I used to transport her favorite gin from her home planet to the Justice Station for years. I'm hoping she'll remember that." He pulled out the bottle of gin he had found at the apartment. "A peace offering to her."

"It's half-empty," said Goggins, disgusted with Stoller's less than perfect gift-giving etiquette.

"I'll get her more later. It's the thought that counts," said Stoller, stuffing the gin back into his coat pocket.

"It's the galaxy credits that count," emphasized Zara.

"Thank you again for the credits," said Stoller with a smile.

He did have a killer smile. I wished I had one, too.

"Charm won't get you everywhere in life," she said.

"I know that, but it has helped me along the way."

I wondered if I could be charming. Maybe Ava would like me more. Stoller could give me a few tips. I certainly couldn't learn those skills from Goggins. I decided to think about that later.

We made it down twenty floors with no problem. But then Stoller spoke up. "I'm not feeling good about getting to the bottom."

"Why's that?" I said as we kept moving forward.

"Just a gut feeling," he replied.

"We've got to keep going," I said.

"I know." He pulled his hat down farther.

"Hey, we're halfway there," said Zara, trying to bolster his confidence level.

Her reassurance certainly didn't bolster mine. I'd reviewed various tactical routes earlier, and there were none more advantageous then heading straight into the area. There were no back exits, elevators or underground tunnels.

I spotted a man in a cape on an adjacent escalator. He was eyeing Stoller and then darted his eyes away when he caught me staring at him.

"Someone just identified Stoller," I said.

Stoller ducked to hide between me, Zara and Goggins.

"Where is he?" asked Goggins.

"On our right. Across the way, black cape," I said.

"Got him," said Zara.

The bounty hunter in the cape veered our way. His escalator was below us, and he saw we were re-positioning. He pulled out his gun and jumped onto another escalator coming up toward us.

"He jumped," said Goggins.

The bounty hunter fired his gun. None of us were hit. Commuters scattered and screamed. I returned fire, as did Zara.

"I don't like this." Stoller crouched.

"What's the alternative?" yelled Goggins.

One my shots hit the bounty hunter, and he fell over the escalator onto another that was traveling down.

"That pretty much blows our cover," said Goggins as he scanned the crowd running away from our direction.

"All we can do is try to beat that bounty hunter down to the main level. He'll be up from the stun in five minutes," I said.

Stoller pulled out the gun he had hidden.

"I thought you weren't carrying?" said Zara.

"I didn't mean to doubt your ability, but well, I doubt everyone's ability but my own. No offense," he said as he threw off his hat.

"When you put it that way. No offense taken," said Goggins.

"You always offend me," snapped Zara.

"Okay, guys, jump!" I lept over the escalator and fell down three floors. I landed hard but made it. I waved for the team to follow.

"Frazzle me. Thanks for the warning, Gabe," said Goggins.

Stoller jumped, then Zara. Goggins hesitated and then dove off the escalator right when another alien bounty hunter started firing from a nearby escalator going up. The alien was small and had two companions. They leaped off their escalator to a downward one that was nearing us.

Stoller and Zara landed their jumps

"Ooof," grunted Goggins as he hit the guardrail hard. He hung by one hand. I grabbed his free hand and pulled him over

"Thanks, Gabe. Ahh."

"Are you all right?" I asked.

"I think so."

"Good, because we need to jump again. Now!" I jumped down another three escalator flights, followed by Stoller and Zara.

"You mechanical misfit. Wait for me!" yelled Goggins as he flung himself over the escalator and landed.

We were heading down fast, with only eight more floors we needed to descend.

"Over there! Two bounty hunters." Stoller pointed upward just as they took aim for us. Stoller got hit in his upper left thigh. He stifled a grunt as he hit the floor. Goggins and I fired back.

Two more bounty hunters on adjacent escalators shot at us.

"They're coming out like fireflies at night," said Goggins.

"On your right, Dr. Goggins," I yelled. He turned and shot at a lone bounty hunter heading down our escalator. That one fell over the guardrails.

"At least he didn't have a long fall," said Goggins.

"How bad?" Zara asked Stoller.

"Bad enough," he replied.

"Can you walk?" I asked.

"Yeah, I think so."

We helped him to his feet.

"I've got you," I said, picking him up and flinging us both down three flights.

"Wha—" he screamed as we plunged down. Zara and Goggins followed. We all hit the next escalator hard but in one piece. A crowd scattered, and I spotted more bounty hunters pointing and aiming at us. Shots rained down on us.

"Five more floors," I said, looking down on the bond auction pit. The bidding had already started for the sol, and the audience was packed with a hundred bounty hunters shoving and waving their comm devices as they bid on skips.

"Two more jumps," I said.

"And then what?" said Stoller as he eyed his wound. His leg was a bit fried but not terrible. Zara tore part of her cape and wrapped the piece of cloth around his leg.

"Thank you," he said to her with a smile.

"I expect two thousand galaxy credits taken off the quinker tally I owe you," she said.

"You got it." He winked.

"I can pretend I'm a bounty hunter and capture you," I said.

"Robots aren't allowed to be bounty hunters," said Stoller. "It's prejudice, I know. But you have to be biological. They'd never believe Goggins is a bounty hunter. I mean, look at him." We all glanced at Goggins. He was right.

"Normally, I would be offended. But I'm not in this instance," said Goggins.

"It has to be Zara," said Stoller as he glanced at her.

"Are you up for that?" I asked.

"I don't think I have a choice," she said.

Stoller laughed. "Just growl a lot. They seem to do that frequently from the run-ins I've had with bounty hunters — male and female."

"Got it — grrr," said Zara.

"Exactly," said Stoller. I grabbed him and leaped down another three flights. Zara and Goggins were right behind me. We were heading down right into the pit of the bond auction. The bounty hunters heard the commotion of shots ringing down on us. They all drew their weapons.

Zara waved her cape in the air as we huddled low on the descending escalator. "Hold it, hold up. This one is mine. I claim him!"

The auctioneer, an insectoid alien, pounded his electronic gavel, bringing the grumbling crowd to a hush.

"Cease fire, cease fire. The bounty huntress has made her claim. Put down your weapons," yelled the auctioneer, who inspected us closely with its multitude of eyes as we made it to the ground floor.

The firing stopped.

Zara stood up and yanked Stoller's neck collar up for all to see she had collared a bail skipper. She waved her gun. The crowd applauded. Goggins and I stood up.

Zara dragged the limping Stoller through the crowd. The grimy but respectful bounty hunters made way for Zara and Stoller. We followed them into the pit.

"That's James Stoller," someone yelled.

Stoller let Zara drag him by the collar. He smiled as he heard his name. "Sorry, hunters. I'm taken." The bounty hunters didn't like that comment, and they started crowding in on him. I pushed some away, and we made our way through the crowd to the other end of the pit. Zara kept up a good charade as she brandished her gun and growled at the other hunters.

I saw a bright neon blue light that flashed *Maxima Sono Bail Bonds* in a storefront window. Another signed blinked *Open* in neon pink. A video of Maxima with galaxy currency signs around her face played in the window. She was large, as Stoller had warned us.

We were approaching her door when another shout came from the pit. "She's not a bounty hunter. That's Stoller's shipmate."

Hundreds of guns pulled from holsters and armed made a deafening noise. We turned to see all their guns pointing at us.

"Oh, boy," gulped Goggins.

"Run!" I yelled, turning to protect my team as Zara, Stoller and Goggins ran to Maxima's store. A looming figure emerged from the shop with the biggest gun I ever saw. It was Maxima. She wielded the bazooka gun and aimed it at the approaching heap of bounty hunters. I backed up behind Maxima.

"Now, everyone stay put. Stoller is on my bond!" she yelled with authority.

The bounty hunters stopped, grumbled and turned back to the bond auction pit.

Maxima studied us over and snarled, "Where the blazes have you been, Stoller?"

"I missed you, but I didn't come empty-handed." He pulled out the still intact, half-drank bottle of gin. She grabbed it and took a swig. Then belched.

Stoller smiled and limped into her office.

Stoller's lawyer Deter sat inside Maxima's office. His legs were crossed, and he was enjoying a cup of coffee. We all took a seat, and Stoller stretched out his injured leg on Maxima's desk.

"Nice to see you, counselor," said Stoller.

"Ditto," said Deter. He took a sip of his beverage. "I'm glad to see you made it relatively unscathed."

"Yeah, piece of cake. And thanks for the bottle of gin."

Maxima came in and slammed her gun and bottle of gin on the desk, which caused Stoller's leg to drop to the floor. He stifled a shout from the pain.

Maxima sat down with a heavy thud and leaned over her desk to Stoller. "Start talking, pretty-boy."

"Have a seat, Maxima — and another drink," said Stoller as he pointed to the bottle. "No reason for us not to be friendly about all this. In fact, I could take a shot right now myself."

"I'm out a lot of money because of you," she said as she swirled her seat behind the desk. "And I'm not going to share a drink with you before I get my galaxy credits. Do you have them?"

"Yes, absolutely." Stoller turned to Zara, who began to reach for her comm device. She couldn't find it.

Goggins and I exchanged a look. This was not good.

Zara patted down all her pockets and her torn cape.

Stoller tried to look calm but kept staring at Zara. "I'm sure you have your comm device somewhere." He winked and smiled at Maxima, who raised an eyebrow to all of us.

"I told you to make sure you had your galaxy credits today," said Deter in a reprimanding tone.

Zara was trying to remember. "I took off my cape and wrapped Stoller's leg. Then I put it—" She snapped her fingers, put her hand on her holster and pulled out her coder. "There it is."

Stoller faked a laugh. Goggins let out a sigh of relief. I grunted. Everyone glanced over at me.

"That's how I laugh," I explained.

"Whatever," said Maxima as she examined me up and down.

"Let me call up the credits," said Zara as she punched a few buttons on her coder and brought up a hologram of the galaxy credits to pay off Stoller's bond. "This should do it." Zara pushed out the credits to Maxima's comm device.

"Plus extra interest for jumping. Ten percent more," said Maxima. She motioned with her hand for Zara to up the amount.

Zara punched a few more buttons and threw more galaxy

credits to Maxima's comm device. Maxima nodded and then grabbed the bottle of gin.

"Now we can drink." She poured shots in four glasses.

Stoller laughed heartily and slapped Zara on the back. "I wasn't worried at all." Zara lurched forward from Stoller's slap and grimaced.

"Honestly, I was, a bit," Zara said.

"I'll drink to that," said Goggins as he grabbed a glass. Stoller handed a glass to Zara and took one for himself.

Deter shook his head. He wasn't drinking. That was a good thing. I wished I could drink in times like these. It was a bonding ritual for humans and aliens that would be nice to partake in, but someone besides our lawyer needed to keep a clear head.

"What should we drink to?" asked Stoller.

"What else? To freedom," said Maxima as she downed her shot.

"To freedom," said Stoller and Zara.

Deter hoisted up his coffee cup and took a drink. "Freedom to all."

"Here, here," said Goggins, who smiled and slammed back his shot, then coughed.

"To freedom," I said, even though I didn't have a shot glass. Everyone stared at me, and I shrugged.

"What is he?" asked Maxima, pointing to me.

"That is Gabe. Robot extraordinaire." Stoller grabbed Deter's untouched shot of gin.

"I hate to break up the party, but we do still have some business at hand," said Deter as he put down his coffee cup.

"Yes. What's next?" said Stoller.

"We have to turn you in to the authorities. Then they will reset your trial date. The judge will either see you as a flight risk and put you in jail or set another bond, which you, I mean Zara, can pay and then await your trial."

Stoller's expression sank. "Jail."

"Let's go," said Deter as he got up.

"Stoller needs medical attention," I said.

"There's a medical facility on the way. We can stop there beforehand," said Deter as he headed out of the office. "Thank you, Maxima. See you soon."

"Yes, nice doing business with you," Maxima yelled. "Good bird, that Deter. Now keep your nose clean, and don't jump bail again."

"Never again," said Stoller.

"Thanks for the gin," said Maxima as she took another shot.

"Thank you for saving my life out there."

"Hasn't been the first time, won't be the last," said Maxima.

"Yes, it will," promised Stoller.

"She saved your life before?" I asked as we followed Deter out of the office.

"Yeah, long story," said Stoller. "I'll tell you over a drink one day."

We all headed out to the medbay, following Deter.

"I'm starting to like it here," said Goggins as he tried to swagger like the other bounty hunters.

"You're nuts," said Zara as she pulled her cape around her shoulder.

I was withholding my personal view of the Justice Station until I saw the robot-judges in action at Stoller's upcoming pre-trial hearing. I hoped the robot-judge could sense Stoller's goodness, even if it was wrapped up in a rough exterior with a tinge of gin splashed on top.

4

Deter led us into the medical facility in the middle hub and helped Stoller check in for treatment on his leg. We took a seat in the reception area. None of us knew what to do with ourselves. I took to people watching. I scanned the area and noticed there were few children in the medbay, and when I thought about it, I hadn't seen more than a handful of children on the whole station.

"Deter, are there many families living on the Justice Station?" I asked.

He tilted his head up from his comm device. "No, not many. I mean, there are plenty of married couples, but having children isn't the highest priority for the workforce on the station."

"That's too bad," I said.

"Why do you say that?" asked Deter. "You can't have children."

A pain hit my chest. "That is correct. But I've had interactions with a few children in the past, and they can bring a lot of joy into one's life."

"And frustration," said Goggins as he thumbed through media on his comm device.

"True," I said. "But I don't think that outweighs the good part. Do you have a family, Deter?"

"No, I don't. I find total enjoyment in my practice. I don't wish to have any children."

Hmmm. I sighed.

"Was that a sigh, Gabe? I didn't know robots sighed. Are you judging me?"

"I apologize. And yes, that was a sigh. Not a judgement of you. I was just thinking," I said.

"Your sentient reactions are fascinating. The robot-judges in the low-level courts are sentient but are not touchy-feely. As you will find out," said Deter.

I didn't view myself as touchy-feely, and it didn't feel good to have Deter view me that way. I put a note in my system to reduce my sigh allotment. "Tell us about the robot-judges," I said.

"You'll get to observe for yourself. I have Stoller's pre-trial hearing scheduled for later today."

"Excellent. Looking forward to it," I said.

"I'm not," said Stoller. "Do they have a sense of humor?"

"No, not at all," said Deter.

"Then I'm in trouble," said Stoller.

The nurse called out Stoller's name, and he stood. "I hope they don't amputate," he said and winked at us.

"Or amputate the wrong thing," said Goggins.

"Yeah. Good point, Doc," said Stoller as he limped to the medbay rooms with the nurse.

"That nurse will have a handful," said Zara.

Goggins craned his neck and browsed the room. I glanced over and saw an older man in a medical uniform talking with a technician.

Goggins nudged Zara with his arm. "Hey, isn't that professor Julipo from University?"

Zara followed his gaze. She smiled.

"Yes, that's him all right. Wow, small galaxy."

"I wonder what he's doing here?" said Goggins.

"Who is Professor Julipo?" I asked.

"Actually, Dr. Julipo. He was our bio-computer systems professor where Zara and I received our doctorates," answered Goggins.

"You know Dr. Julipo? He's one of my clients." Deter turned and waved the doctor over to us.

"I wonder if he heard my doctorate was stripped," Zara whispered to Goggins.

"I doubt it. He left the university years ago to start his own private practice developing human enhancements," said Goggins.

"He makes cyborgs?" I asked, leaning in.

"Yes, but legal ones. He's a good man," said Goggins.

"I wonder if he's involved with the Supreme Court justices' transition to robots," I said.

"You mean collaborating with Ameribot Industries?" said Goggins.

Dr. Julipo noticed Deter waving to him, smiled, and toddled over to us. Deter offered his hand, and Dr. Julipo shook it in a friendly matter.

"Deter, good to see you. You're not sick, are you?" asked Dr. Julipo.

"No, healthy as a bird can be."

"Hello, Dr. Julipo, do you remember us?" asked Zara, smiling. I hadn't seen Zara smile too many times. It was nice to see.

"Your favorite students from long ago," said Goggins, straightening up in his seat.

Dr. Julipo snapped his fingers, trying to remember their names. "I do. I do. Zara and Cecil. Why, it's been too long," he said, delighted with his former students.

Goggins and Zara laughed. "So good to see you, Doctor," said Zara.

"What are you doing at the Justice Station?" asked Goggins.

"Can you keep a secret?" said Dr. Julipo as he looked left and right.

"I don't know if we should discuss —" started Deter, but Dr. Julipo interrupted him.

"I trust these folks. They were my best students." He took a seat with us. "I received a subcontract from Ameribot Industries to work on the Supreme Court justices. You've heard about them, haven't you?"

"The human justices are retiring and being replaced by robots, correct?" replied Goggins.

"Yes, but more than that," said Dr. Julipo. "We finalized brokering a deal with the justices. That's why I have engaged Deter here."

"What kind of deal?" asked Zara.

"We are in discussions to upload their actual consciousnesses into the robots. Isn't that exciting? Totally galaxy-breaking work. I may win a BioTech Galaxy award over this and get more funding," said an excited Dr. Julipo.

All of us were a bit stunned. Zara and Goggins sat back in their chairs, absorbing the news.

Goggins was able to stammer a few words out. "That is incredible. Congratulations."

"Don't congratulate me yet. We haven't performed the operation. But I am hopeful."

"I thought the premise of having robot-judges was that they're impartial and incorruptible since they have no human ties or any ways to be prejudice or persuaded by emotions or bribery," said Zara.

"Yes. That is working fine for the robot-judges in the lower courts. But these are Supreme Court justices ruling over our entire galaxy. And these are the most noble three justices we have had in centuries," he explained.

I nudged Goggins.

"Ow. Dr. Julipo. This is, um, Gabe. Zara and I are his creators," said Goggins. I gave him a hard stare. I guess he had to explain me somehow and couldn't tell his professor I was created by Ava and Damiel Kell at Ameribot Industries. I'd just have to go with it.

"Hello," I said.

"Hello there," said Dr. Julipo as he leaned in to study me. "Are you sentient?"

"Yes, I am," I replied.

"Fascinating," said Dr. Julipo. "Wonderful job."

"Thank you," said Goggins as he smirked at me and shrugged his shoulders.

"Dr. Julipo, to get back to Zara's question. Aren't you afraid that the Supreme Court justices with their consciousnesses in the robots, will still be corruptible, even if they never were in the past? The potentiality is still there," I said.

Dr. Julipo cocked his head and laughed. "There is potentiality in anything. And I don't have to tell you that since you most likely already computed this and are gently asking me if there are any risks that I am worried about."

I liked him, even though he may be entering down a very fraught-filled path.

He moved his attention back to Zara and Goggins. "Gee, you really did a wonderful job with Gabe." He shifted his focus back to me. "I'm not fearful, but we are going to thoroughly vet the justices tomorrow in my lab here."

"Really?" asked Zara. "Will there be any Ameribot Industries leaders there?"

"Only the lead engineer. His name is Redford. Nice fellow."

"I never heard of him. I mean, is he a long-time Ameribot employee?" asked Goggins.

"No, as a matter of fact. He just graduated from University. Top-notch doctoral student."

"How nice," said Goggins. "That's good."

"Say, would you two consider assisting me on this project? I could use the help. You were my top students and look what you've accomplished with Gabe," said the beaming doctor.

"Yes. We would be honored," said Zara.

I nudged Goggins again in the ribs. "And Gabe is our lab assistant. He would be most helpful, too."

"Of course. Wonderful," said Dr. Julipo. "Meet me at the lab tomorrow morning. Deter needs to be there for some legal paperwork with the justices, so he can show you the way."

Deter's comm device went off. He motioned to us that he had to take a call and stepped away.

Dr. Julipo rose and bowed slightly as he bid goodbye. "How serendipitous to run into you here. I never asked what you are doing here."

Goggins and Zara stared blankly at each other. Then Goggins winked.

"We're getting married—and we are just finalizing the pre-nup with Deters," said Goggins. Zara's mouth dropped open.

"How wonderful. And why are you in the medbay?" asked Dr. Julipo, concerned.

Goggins turned to Zara for that answer. The suspense was killing me on what Zara would say.

"Our minister, Reverend Stoller, took a stumble and hurt his leg when we were in the wedding rehearsal. And Deter was helpful and directed us here," said Zara.

Wow. Okay. That was good. Reverend Stoller.

"Until tomorrow. See you then. And congratulations. I hope I get an invite to the wedding since I'm here for a few weeks."

"Me too. I mean, certainly." Goggins waved goodbye.

Dr. Julipo turned to leave, and Zara punched Goggins in the arm.

"Oww," Goggins howled.

"Marriage. Wedding? What came over you?" said a very upset Zara.

"What? I thought it was very clever. Right, Gabe?"

"It wasn't bad," I replied.

Stoller came out of the back office with his leg wrapped, walking with a limp. The nurse patted him on the back in a friendly manner, and Stoller continued to chat with her.

"Stoller," said Goggins as he watched him flirt with the nurse.

"Don't you mean, Reverend Stoller?" I asked.

Goggins gave me a hard glance. "Really, Gabe. I'd think you would be more respectful to your co-creator."

I grunted. "Anyway, thank you for getting us into the lab tomorrow. I believe the Heragi Empire could be corrupting the justices' operation to become robots."

"Agreed," said Zara. "And I don't know how I feel about putting human consciousnesses into robots."

"If it is legitimate, then its ground-breaking work. But if the Heragi Empire can somehow control the justices' consciousnesses and thus the outcomes of planetary court cases, then that is trouble for the whole galaxy," said Goggins.

"What'd I miss?" asked a confused Stoller.

"Nothing, Reverend," said Zara with a smile.

"What did she mean by that?" he asked.

"Never mind," said Goggins.

Deter strode over to us and glanced at Stoller. "You look better. Ready to go meet your robot-judge?"

"Can't wait," said Stoller as he slapped Deter on the back and limped out of the medbay. He was in a better mood. I had to think that perhaps the nurse had given him a tranquilizer which may not have been a bad thing.

We waited in a small courtroom that had a whole wall of windows looking out into deep space. Stoller nervously tapped his knee as he sat at the defender's table with Deter. Goggins,

Zara and I sat in the gallery with others who were awaiting their trial dates and bond amounts.

The robot-judge hadn't arrived yet. I surveyed the courtroom. The bailiff was an alien species I wasn't familiar with, so I did a bio-scan and also took a pic of their face to load into my alien directory. My alien directory pulled up a match—the bailiff was from an edger planet called Eaps, and its species had the same name. It was an Eap. It was magenta in color, with four hands and a powerful build which I presumed was helpful when dealing with criminals and alleged criminals who were hostile for being called criminals.

Glancing over at the judge's empty desk, I read its name-plate. *The Honorable Ronni* was the name of the robot-judge presiding in courtroom 691. Ronni didn't have a last name iden-tified, just like me or any robot. We were typically called by our registration and series name or an acronym, if we were lucky.

Lucky? Where did that come from? I felt a bit of resentment that robots didn't have last names or full names. Of course, nanny-bots were given pet names by their owners, but it would be nice to have a full name like humans are given at birth. We are birthed too, in a way.

There was something bothering me.

I took a minute to review my system and the present situa-tion. Ever since I heard about robotic Supreme Court justices, it rubbed me the wrong way. I could understand the logic of utilizing robots as judges. And in the lower courts, it certainly made sense.

The number of legal cases over a couple of thousand years is impossible to track, so having robots that can assess a case and look at just the facts to determine an outcome if it's innocence or a sentence for the defendant seemed like a correct historical, legal and technological advancement for the galaxy. Fair for the edger worlds and for the Heragi Empire.

I sighed. Zara glanced over at me. I re-calibrated my system again to reduce the number of sighs I released. A pain hit my chest. There was something wrong about all of this, beyond the threat that I felt from the Heragi Empire trying to influence the robots that Ameribot made for the justices. I just needed to put my finger on it.

The door to the judge's chambers opened. The bailiff stood up, as did everyone in the courtroom.

"All rise for the honorable Judge Ronni," called out the bailiff.

Judge Ronni was dressed in the customary blue gauze robes of the Zephon galaxy courts. I had never seen a human judge, so it was hard to compare to how different a robot-judge was in comparison. But I was able to review the judge-robot as a robot. I scanned its face and any external showing of armor or appendages.

Its frame wasn't much different than mine. A few inches shorter and less armor. I imagined its CPU was fast, and actually, it could have been an older model since robot-judges on the lower courts had been in place for the past five years.

Judge Ronni pounded its hologram gavel in the air, and it sounded two rings that silenced the courtroom murmurs.

"Rothworth vs. Stoller is the first case on the docket," announced the bailiff.

The judge tilted its head, and code rolled in its eyes. Interesting. I enlarged my view of its head to get a closer view. It must be wired into the whole Justice Station legal directory. In fact, it could be remotely tied into the whole legal galaxy directory.

"Did you see that?" whispered Zara.

"Yes, not a comforting look," said Goggins.

"Counselor Deter Finz, I see that your client has paid the bond he skipped on," said Judge Ronni.

Deter rose. "Yes, Judge." He is staying at my apartment on the station, so I can assure he is an extremely low flight risk."

The judge nodded.

Stoller stood up. Deter tried to push him down into his seat.

"What is he doing?" whispered Zara.

"This could be bad," I said.

"Judge, Judge, if I may?" said Stoller.

"You have something to say, Mr. Stoller?" asked Judge Ronni.

Deter shook his feathered head, disappointed in Stoller.

"Yes, Judge. I just want to say that this whole case is a travesty. Jessio Rothworth lost the starship in a card game we were playing and, if I'm under oath I have to say, he's pretty bad at quinker. And an even bigger sore loser."

"Blazes," said Goggins as he lowered his head. "This is a disaster."

"Really?" said the judge. "And that is why you skipped your bail?"

"I, um. I just thought we could save a lot of time if this case never saw the light of our sol, that's all."

"Do you plan on having any witnesses at your trial, Mr. Stoller?"

"Witnesses? Do I have to?"

In a last-ditch effort, Deter bit Stoller on the arm with his beak and shoved him down into his chair.

"Ah!" yelled Stoller. That must have hurt, but it did the trick. Stoller rubbed his arm and quieted down.

"Judge, my apologies. My client can call witnesses if that is needed, but to get back to the bond setting, he is ready to see the case through."

"That is very thoughtful of him. I won't be setting a bail amount on him, Mr. Deter."

"Thank you, Judge," said Deter, wiping his beak with a handkerchief. He was certainly earning his galaxy credits.

"And that is because he will be spending his time in jail until the case is held in three days." The judge pounded his gavel twice. "We will see you all then. The court administrators will notify Jessio Rothworth, so he can appear if he wishes. Good sol."

Deter lowered his head in defeat.

"What? I'm going to jail? Deter!" Stoller yelled while the bailiff escorted him away.

"Blasters," said Goggins, shaking his head.

Stoller swung his head back at us, but he had no words for once in his life. We watched them take him away.

Deter turned and shook his head at us. I actually felt sorry for the avian lawyer. This was his first time dealing with Stoller in a tense situation. I had been through a few of those with Stoller, and he was a wild card. I hoped that Deter prepared a good case in the short amount of time he had.

We all got up and left the courtroom, a bit stunned.

"Poor Stoller," said Zara.

"Poor Stoller? I feel sorry for his cell mate. That person will be up all night listening to him complain," said Goggins.

Deter hung his head. "That didn't go as planned."

"You *will* win the case, right?" asked Zara.

"Yes. I mean, I have every intention to — if I can keep Stoller from speaking," said Deter. They all headed out of the courtroom as I stayed behind and watched the robot-judge at his desk. Then Judge Ronni's head turned toward me as I was walking out. He noticed I was scanning his system. He nodded at me. I nodded back and marched out of the courtroom.

5

———————

We gathered inside an observatory room on the top hub of the Justice Station near the Supreme Court offices. Deter's security pass cleared me, Goggins and Zara for entry. The room was impressive which was a different feel from the skip auction pit on the first floor. Tall windows showcased deep space from floor to ceiling, and the floor deck had see-through glass. You almost felt like you were floating outside into the Edge.

All of us stared out into the beauty of space. None of us spoke. It was regal and needed reverence. After a few moments, Deter ushered us into the nearby conference room with an equally impressive view. Dr. Julipo was already seated and waiting for us. "Welcome, welcome. So glad you are here to assist."

"Hello, Doctor," said Goggins and Zara.

Dr. Julipo said, "Hello, Gabe."

"Hello," I responded. He seemed to be giddy every time I replied to him. He must have robot-fever. I felt like I had a fan. He smiled and I nodded to him.

"The weight of the importance of this court is palpable in this room," said Goggins.

Deter took a seat. "As it should be. In the Zephon Galaxy, we have endured hundreds of years of planetary wars and fierce battles among its inhabitants, but this galactic Supreme Court has survived. And these last three human Supreme Court justices are the most trusted and revered."

"So you said before," said Zara. "Why now?

"I can answer that," said Dr. Julipo. "The justices are older and having health challenges. They're sick. They have been for years."

"What? I've read no news stories about that," said Goggins.

"No, and you never will. But it is true. Hence the work over the past few years to expedite the robot-judges on the lower courts, to work out the bugs, if you will."

"And they didn't want to elect new human or alien judges to replace them? As is customary?" I asked.

"There was a detailed study. The social scientists polled hundreds of thousands of galactic citizens. The current judges were viewed as the most fair, honest and intelligent justices in the past three hundred years. The recommendation was to sustain the citizens' peace of mind and keep these particular judges — forever," he explained.

"Who wrote the study?" I asked.

"More importantly, who funded the study?" asked Zara. Always follow the money, Zara often said.

"The Heragi Empire, to answer both your questions," Dr. Julipo.

"And you don't think they had any ulterior motive?" asked Zara.

"No. None of the Supreme Court justices are Heragians." Dr. Julipo poured a glass of water.

"But Ameribot Industries is based on Heragi, and they built the justices' robotic bodies," said Goggins.

"Yes, but it was a blind bidding process," said Deter.

"The lower court robot-judges don't have human conscious-nesses," said Zara.

"Correct, but it was deemed necessary for the Supreme Court. With careful mediation led by Deter, we treaded softly and asked the justices if they were interested in, well, being immortal justices," said Dr. Julipo as he gulped down his water.

Deter nodded. "Yes, and after careful consideration, they agreed."

Immortal justices. Immortal. My chest hurt. That was what was bothering me. I touched my chest.

"Are you okay, Gabe?" asked Goggins.

"Yes, fine."

"How can we help you today, Dr. Julipo?" asked Zara.

"Be astute observers. This the final round of a series of psychological questions to make sure they are ready. The surgery is scheduled for tomorrow. They may have more questions or a change of heart. This is forever," he said.

Indeed.

The door opened and a security-bot stepped in. It was armed with a gun on its holster. It swept the room and then nodded to someone in the hallway.

The three Supreme Court justices filed into the room. The security-bot exited. I assumed it would be posted outside to prevent any intruders.

Dr. Julipo and Deter were the first ones to stand up. Goggins, Zara and I jumped to our feet too. We were rusty with our galactic dignitary protocols. Dr. Julipo shook the justices' hands. Deter nodded and offered his greetings.

They wore matching green tunics. Their pace was slow, as one would expect of someone their age. They seemed fragile, but their eyes were sharp. Dr. Julipo pulled out the seat for each one of them. Either old age or some kind of illness had slowed them down. I scanned their bio-metric levels, which were low but stable.

Dr. Julipo stood at the head of the table. "Justices, thank you for our final meeting today before the surgery tomorrow. Let me introduce the new faces you see here today. I've asked former university colleagues to join me. We have Dr. Zara Lorgia and Dr. Cecil Goggins and their lab assistant, Gabe. They made him. He is fully sentient," said the proud professor.

"Zara, Cecil and Gabe. This is the Justice Tefara Kimathi."

She was bald and her skin was gold. I ran a scan of her against my alien directory. Her green eyes were striking, and she smiled at us all. A match came back that she was from the planet Uvens. We returned her nod.

"And this is Justice Guy Cadiux."

He was small, with three eyes and scales. The hue of his skin was orange, and my alien directory reported he was from the planet Mybeler.

"Hello, nice to meet you," said Guy. We replied back the same.

"And this is Chief Justice Lilou Parado," said Dr. Julipo as he sat down.

She was an Oliverian, seven feet tall, and had the same features as General Anjori Oliverian, who I had met on another mission. Lilou gave us a slight smile as she studied each of us. Her eyes were blue, like Ava's.

"Today we will conclude our final interview regarding the uploading of your consciousnesses to the robotic constructs that were uniquely created by Ameribot Industries for this occasion," said Dr. Julipo.

"Yes, Doctor, we are ready," said Lilou. The other justices nodded in agreement.

"Good, and thank you, Lilou. Let's discuss if any of you are having last minute questions, regrets or even fears. You can talk candidly. There is no embarrassment about feeling cautious or even trepidatious." Dr. Julipo he took off his glasses.

It was a good question. Dr. Julipo was trying to make sure

the justices were ready for the upcoming operation and for the rest of their lives.

The room was silent for a few seconds.

Tefara was the first to speak up. "Dr. Julipo, we know you have been perfecting the surgery over the past few weeks. We had a conversation this morning, amongst ourselves, and we do have a few questions."

"Certainly, ask away."

Guy started. "First, what will happen if something goes wrong? Is that then the end of the person?"

"Yes and no," said Dr. Julipo. "If the robotics fails or the operation fails, we won't be able to put you back into your body. But we were recently able to develop a back-up system, if you may. Your consciousness will be on an intermediary chip that we can save and perhaps try again at a later date."

The justices turned to each other. Lilou nodded to Guy, who said, "Thank you. Based on your answer, our wishes are that if the surgery or robotic structure fails right after surgery, that you destroy the chip."

Dr. Julipo's head shot up. He was surprised. He then absorbed their answer and nodded. He glanced over to Deter, who also nodded. "Yes, absolutely. You have my promise."

"Another question," said Tefara. "If any one of us would like to stop being a justice in the future, who will replace us?"

Deter answered this question. "The Galactic Council has a playbook. It's an organizational process on that scenario. They will meet and nominate a human judge to the Supreme Court."

The justices nodded.

Interesting and thoughtful questions. I studied each justice's face to discern worry, regret or sadness.

"Please proceed with your questions, Dr. Julipo," said Lilou.

"After the surgery, even if it is months or years in the future and you believe that there is a malfunction or you are not feeling right or cannot perform your duty, do you all remember the procedure we would like you to follow?"

"We will contact the Galactic Council's Chairman of Judicial Proceedings," said Guy.

"Correct. And of course, I will assist in any way I can," said Dr. Julipo.

"And when you die, Doctor? Who will take your place?" asked Tefara.

Dr. Julipo pushed his glasses farther up onto his nose. "I will have named a successor to the program, and that person will do the same, and so on and so on."

"For centuries?" asked Guy.

"Why, yes."

"Do you believe the robots' parts or mechanics will last for centuries?" asked Lilou.

"I believe so. And if they don't, Ameribot will figure out a replacement, perhaps."

"Perhaps?" asked Lilou.

"I mean, succinctly, they will, and they can remove your consciousness from the robot and move it to another robot."

"Good. That is what we were hoping you would confirm," said Lilou with a gentle smile.

"And have you all notified your immediate family members regarding this surgery? This may be psychologically traumatic and jarring for them too," Dr. Julipo asked.

They all said *yes*.

"Any issues?"

They all said *no*.

"Is anyone having any nightmares or insomnia due to the upcoming surgery?"

They all shook their heads *no*.

Guy leaned forward. "What will happen if, let's say, a mishap happens, and my consciousness evaporates or stops in some manner? Will the robot be able to continue on its own without any outside party knowing this?"

Dr. Julipo waited a moment to answer. "The robot will have lost your consciousness, so they will not be able to function. So, if your consciousness dies, then it dies. It will shut down."

There was a pause in the conversation.

"Dr. Julipo?" I asked.

He was startled that I spoke, as was everyone in the room except Lilou. She turned and smiled at me.

"May I ask a question?"

"Yes, of course, Gabe. You may offer a unique perspective."

"Thank you," I said. "Have you all considered loneliness?"

"How so?" asked Guy.

"The loneliness of living forever."

They contemplated my question.

"Are you saying that all robots experience loneliness?" asked Tefara.

"I don't know about all robots. But there is that potential for humans. When all your friends and family pass away," I said.

"We will always have the passion of the law," said Guy as he eyed his colleagues.

"True," I said.

"And our friendship. The three of us are like siblings," said Tefara.

I stared at Lilou, the chief justice. Her blue eyes penetrated me. "Yes, I have thought of that. And yes, we may be lonely," she said. "Are you lonely?"

"Yes, I have been. But, for now, I have my friends," I said.

"And you can continue to make more friends," said Guy. "Just like we will."

"You're right, Justice Cadiux," I replied.

I had said enough. I thought they all knew what I was trying to get across. At least, I believed Lilou did. They could think about it overnight. I was sure there would be a go or no-go discussion right before the surgery. And if that was not planned for, I would suggest it to Dr. Julipo.

"That is all, Doctor," I said.

"Thank you, Gabe. Cecil or Zara, do you have questions?"

"Have you met your robots yet?" asked Zara.

"Not yet. We are looking forward to it," said Tefara with a smile.

"Will they look like us?" asked Guy.

"No, they will not," said Dr. Julipo. "Unfortunately."

"That is not unfortunate," said Guy with a laugh.

I was glad the conversation got uplifted. I was afraid I had dragged down the room. It was good to see Tefara and Guy laugh. I peered back to Lilou, who was gazing at me. Actually, she was studying me.

"I have a question. How long have you all known each other?" asked Goggins.

They all laughed and tried to remember the year. "It was ninety years ago. Lilou was appointed before us. Then I was appointed. And then Tefara," explained Guy.

"And do you always agree? I mean, I heard you have not been divided in a court decision since you have been on the same court," said Goggins.

Guy and Tefara deferred to Lilou.

"That is true. We have agreed on all of our many cases. It's not that we haven't discussed and asked questions, but overall, we are very—how would you say it? Simpatico," she said with a tender smirk.

"Then why should there be three of you? Why not one?" I asked.

"Gabe," said Goggins under his breath.

"There have always been three," said Zara.

I could tell they were both embarrassed by my question. I was familiar with the Supreme Court always having three justices.

Dr. Julipo tried to hide his laugh. He was amused.

Deter didn't like the question at all, and I saw him roll his eyes.

The justices also smirked.

"I'll handle this one," said Lilou to her colleagues. "Gabe, I know you must already have complete details of our galaxy judicial processes. You may know it better than most in this room." There were more giggles from everyone. "For argument's sake, you may have a point to consider. For us, there is still a potential to be divided, but it is not probable, and hence there has been and forever will be three justices. But you know that already. What is your real question? That is what I would like to know."

I leaned forward. "Could the Supreme Court go on with only one justice?"

"No," she snapped back quickly.

"Why?" I asked.

She paused and stared directly into my eyes. "The weight of these decisions is heavy, and it's too much for human shoulders, perhaps even robotic shoulders, and needs to be shared amongst us three," said Lilou.

I nodded.

"Is that the answer you were wanting to hear?" she asked.

"I had no expectation. I was just curious. Thank you."

"A curious robot," she said.

My mind drifted to the future. Beyond loneliness, there is foreverness. You can't outrun it. It just has to play out. And a robot at some point has to face that, at least sentient robots. This was what the three Supreme Court justices would feel when they got their consciousnesses put in the robotic structures. And I would guess the emotional pain would be greater for them, for they were once human and would have many friends and family members to miss.

"If there are no more questions from anyone, then I think we have completed our meeting. Anyone? No? Deter, you are next," said Dr. Julipo.

"Yes," said Deter as he brought up a hologram picture of a contract from his comm device. "Justices, we need your confirmation and signatures. This final contract states that you agree to the surgery and do not hold Dr. Julipo, Ameribot Industries or the Galactic Council responsible for any liability if anything goes wrong."

The justices reviewed the hologram document.

"We are giving you permission to proceed with the surgery, but we will not sign that document," said Guy as they all stood up to leave.

"I mean, really, Deter, we are lawyers, too," said Tefara. They all laughed and saw themselves out of the room.

"Of course, you are," said Deter. He stood up and bowed as they left.

"That went wonderful," said Goggins with an eye roll.

"Ameribot won't be happy about them not signing. But that won't stop the surgery," said Deter, shaking his head.

"What do you think?" Dr. Julipo asked Zara and Goggins.

"I think they are so well-adjusted that they are too adjusted. Does that make sense?" said Zara.

"I know what you mean," said Dr. Julipo. "They almost act now like one mind. And I think that is what you were getting at Gabe, weren't you?"

"Yes, Doctor," I said. He was quite bright.

"I think they are ready. As ready as anyone could be on the precipice of being immortal," said Goggins.

"Any last concerns?" asked Dr. Julipo.

"Not for them," said Zara.

"Let me guess. Ameribot?" said Dr. Julipo.

"Yes," said Goggins. "They are the weak link."

"They are the *corrupt* link," I emphasized.

"I respect you all, but I have been working with Dr. Redford, and he is very respectful," said Dr. Julipo.

"We understand," said Zara.

"When will the robots be here?" I asked.

"Tomorrow," said Deter.

"With Dr. Redford," said Dr. Julipo. "I need to tell you all that the pressure of this surgery and timeline are enormous."

"We're happy to support you, Dr. Julipo," said Zara. "We just want to make sure the justices are safe."

"That the galaxy will be safe," I said.

"Okay, then we have the same intention," said Dr. Julipo, turning to Deter.

"Agreed," said Deter.

"And Dr. Julipo, Deter, we need to tell you why we aren't exactly fans of Ameribot Industries and vice versa," said Goggins.

"Please tell," said Deter.

Goggins and Zara went on explaining our experience with CEO Manstine, Drs. Ava and Damiel Kell and their children. I stayed quiet. I enjoyed hearing them tell the story. It was much more enjoyable to listen to it than to think back on it. Humans have a way of skipping over the hard parts and just relaying the good parts. I preferred it that way too.

But they could only tell their viewpoints. Individually.

They didn't know how I felt. Or how I felt about everyone. About Ava.

And it was better that way.

The next sol, Deter met us at the jail to visit Stoller.

The guard-bots delivered Stoller in handcuffs to the visitor cell. Shuffling in, he looked more rough than normal with dark circles under his eyes. He probably hadn't slept a wink. He grinned when he saw us and sat down at our table.

"Morning," said Goggins. "Good to see you."

"You look like you could use a drink," said Zara.

"Did you bring any?" he asked.

"Sorry, no," she said with a shrug.

Stoller let out a sad sigh. "So, Deter, what's the plan?"

"You need witnesses. Are there any we can contact to testify on your behalf?" asked Deter.

Stoller gazed up to the ceiling as he thought. "Yeah, there were two others playing with us."

"Who are they?" asked Deter.

"A pilot who hangs out in the Blue Edger bar on Charbeaux Station. Her name is Fargo. And then there's a gold hunter named Holin. Who knows where he is? But someone in the Blue Edger may know his last whereabouts."

"I heard that Jessio Rothworth will be arriving at the Justice Station soon," said Deter.

"If I win, does he go to jail?"

"No," replied Deter.

"If I lose, do I have to give the ship back to Jessio?"

"Yes, and there could be a possibility of jail time if you lose," said Deter.

Stoller bounced up from his seat. "Why did I even think this was a good idea in the first place? I should have never come here."

"It's always a good idea to clear your name," said Zara.

"Really? Are you going to turn all your money back to the Suisseys?"

Zara went quiet. She turned her eyes away and didn't answer.

"Sorry, forget I said that," said Stoller.

"I forget everything you say immediately," said Zara with a shrug.

"Clever girl," he said under his breath. He glanced over to me. "And what are you looking so glum about, Gabe?"

"I look glum?" I asked.

"I can tell. I've hung around you long enough to know. What? Did Ava send you another hate message or something?"

A pain shot into my chest. "No." Although, that would make me glum.

"Stoller, we're your friends. And you're treating us pretty poorly," said Goggins. "We're all you got."

Stoller rubbed his chin. "Sorry, sorry. I just hate being cooped up like this."

"We know it's tough. Deter will find your witnesses," I said.

"Okay." He sat down again, a bit less agitated. "Now, what is bothering you, Gabe?"

"We met with the Supreme Court justices yesterday," I said.

"Are they helping with my case?" asked Stoller.

"No, you blasted narcissist," yelled Zara.

"You think I'm a narcissist?"

"Listen, we ran into one of our university professors at the medbay while you were being checked out. He asked for us to help interview the justices," said Goggins.

"And we will be assisting in the surgery," added Zara. "The justices' consciousnesses are going to be uploaded into robots created by Ameribot Industries."

"And yes, you do show some moderate narcissistic tendencies," said Goggins.

"The justices need to know there's more than just — boom — your brain is now in this robot. It's just bigger than they think," I said.

"They are wiser than all of us. And smarter. They know what they're getting themselves into," said Deter.

"Will you be able to inspect the robots before and after the surgery?" asked Stoller.

"We're going to try," said Zara.

The robot-guard came back into the room. "Time's up."

"I can see you have your mind on bigger things than me," said Stoller with a downturned face.

"We're not forgetting about you," said Zara.

"Yeah, yeah. Bigger fish to fry. I get it," said Stoller as he headed for the door. Then he turned back. "You know, Jessio Rothworth owns a robot company. He's a jerk and bad at quinker. But he probably hates Ameribot, too." The robot-guard took Stoller's arm and led him out the door.

"Jessio's company is called Roth Robots. They were one of the vendors that lost the robot contract to Ameribot," said Deter.

"How do you know? I thought it was a secret bidding process," said Goggins.

Deter shrugged. "I know people on the Galactic Council."

"Jessio will have a vested interest in helping us," said Zara.

"You can't accuse Ameribot of anything until you have proof," warned Deter.

"I hope we don't find anything wrong with the robots. But we do need access to them," said Goggins.

"We'll get it," I said.

"I'll start working on getting Stoller's witnesses." Deter got up to leave. "Let me know if anything comes up."

"Will do. Thanks, Deter," said Zara.

"Yeah, you're not all that bad, for a lawyer," said Goggins. Deter shot him a glance.

"Just kidding." He held his hands up in jest.

"You'll get used to him," Zara said.

"No, I won't," said Deter as he left the room.

Goggins, Zara and I strolled through the atrium in the central hub. They ordered food at one of the cafes. We watched the workers and visitors hustling up and down the escalators, coming and going to the lawyer offices and courtrooms.

"They all have such faith," I said as I watched everyone rush by us.

"Faith in what?" said Goggins.

"Faith in the galaxy's legal system. When it is one operation away from being changed forever. For better or worse," I said.

"They want to believe. They need to in order to keep balance in their worlds," said Zara.

"It's a shared belief. It must be," added Goggins.

"We need to check the justice robots' prime directive in their CPUs," I said.

"Copy that," said Zara.

"We don't know if Ameribot's Dr. Redford will let us inspect the robots," said Goggins as he took a bite out of his meal.

"Whether he lets us or not, we have to get into their code," I said. "I think we should contact Damiel and Ava Kell."

"Not yet. We need proof. Like Deter told us," said Goggins.

"He's right," said Zara. "We could be worrying over nothing."

"Is that what you think? What you really think?" I asked them both.

"No," said Zara.

"No," said Goggins. "But I don't want to end up in jail like Stoller."

"If it's there, we'll get the proof," I said.

Minni, Deter's robotic bird, flew past us. I watched it head toward his office. I hoped Deter was having good luck finding Stoller's witnesses. We would need him sprung from jail as soon as possible if the judicial robots had been tampered with.

Later, we met Dr. Julipo at the medbay front desk.

"Let's head back to the lab. We have a surgical room set up," he said.

I followed behind the doctor as he led the way. He kept looking back at me and smiling. His crush was making me uncomfortable.

"Is there something you want to ask me, Dr. Julipo?"

"Why, yes. Yes, there is, Gabe. How intuitive of you to know."

We reached the lab and he opened up the door. I entered, and I felt like I was home. It reminded me of the lab back at Ameribot Industries. It was spacious, with similar if not the exact equipment that Ava, Damiel and Goggins used on me and the other bots they created and tested.

"This is a very nice set up, Doctor," said Goggins.

"Yes, we like it. Much of it was sent over from Ameribot."

Dr. Julipo approached me and asked me his question. "Do you dream at night?"

I was surprised by his question. I thought it would be about my CPU speed or pain sensors. But to ask me if I dreamed, it perplexed me, perhaps he was concerned that the justices would have sleep issues.

"No, I don't," I said. "You see, I don't sleep."

"You don't have to be recharged?"

"No, I have a harmonic renewable battery."

"Fascinating," said Dr. Julipo.

"Doctor, I assume you have had test subjects for this operation. That the justices won't be the first humans who have had their consciousnesses uploaded to a robot, correct?"

"Yes. Of course," he said. "We have been experimenting for two years now. But we really only made great strides when Dr. Redford came aboard."

"What happened with the test patients?" asked Zara as she pulled out her coder and was setting up her desk.

"To be honest, a few died, a few went insane and two are thriving."

"Really? Where are the two?" asked Goggins as he inspected the computer equipment.

"One, I believe, is working in the Heragi military."

"How surprising," said Zara with a raise of her eyebrow.

"And the other?" I asked.

Then the door of the lab opened. A robot marched in. It was by itself. It scanned the room and waved at Dr. Julipo. "Hello, Doctor."

Dr. Julipo turned and waved back. "Hello, Dr. Redford. I was just talking about you. You see — Dr. Redford *is* the other test patient."

Goggins, Zara and I stared at Dr. Redford.

He turned to us and bowed. "Nice to meet you. Introductions, please."

It was like I was staring in a mirror. Except for a different coloring of metal — it was a dark black — Dr. Redford had my same physique and armor.

Dr. Julipo made the introductions. Knowing that Goggins'

and even Zara's name would call up red flags when Dr. Redford would certainly cross-reference their names against the Ameribot Industries employee name directories, Zara had gone in and wiped them from all Ameribot and Heragi Empire directories she could find.

"Yes, these are former colleagues of mine from my university. This is Dr. Cecil Goggins, and this is Dr. Zara Lorgia. They will be assisting me in the surgery," he said.

I knew exactly what Dr. Redford was doing. I could see he was checking his internal records and most likely connecting with the computers in the lab to get a link back on his ship to see if there were any red flags on their names. His initial feedback would not give him any information to be concerned about, but if he went back later to dig deeper on Goggins and Zara, he may find their records.

His head turned slightly. He came back from his directory search. It was a slight hint of being offline or distracted. Only I would have caught on to it. He nodded. No red flags.

"Nice to meet you," said Dr. Redford.

"And this is Gabe, their lab assistant."

Dr. Redford studied me up and down. "It seems we have a similar build. Ameribot?"

Goggins stepped in. "Yes, we sourced the materials from Ameribot. Isn't that funny?" Goggins tried to laugh. Zara joined in.

"Gabe is sentient. But no consciousness," said Goggins.

Ow! My chest hurt from that comment. I wondered if Goggins said that only for Dr. Redford or really believed I possessed no consciousness? Could I even argue with him that I did have one? At least I believed I had one. I must have one. I felt pain, so I must have consciousness. All robots did. It's just, not all humans knew that.

"Nice to meet you," I said. He recorded my voice. Or at least

I would have done that if I were him, to try to get any further matching identities later.

"No offense, but Dr. Julipo, I assume you did security checks on your colleagues? To make sure all the security control paperwork is in order."

"Yes. I can send those over to you later. No offense taken. We must be absolutely sure we have integrity and security with the surgery," said Dr. Julipo, who turned and gave Zara a worried look. Goggins' and Zara's professor just took a risk that surprised me. He was sticking his neck out. Zara could provide him with some forged paperwork later to satisfy Dr. Redford. But I made note that perhaps Dr. Julipo shared concerns about the Heragi Empire more than he was letting on. For surely, working with us put him at risk for losing what I would assume was a very lucrative contract with Ameribot. And, of course, his reputation.

"Dr. Redford, we would like to start by asking a few questions about your recovery after the surgery," said Goggins.

"Certainly," said Dr. Redford as he took a seat.

"First, how did you come around to volunteering for the surgery? You could have met a fate like the others," asked Zara.

"That is why I volunteered. I didn't want to subject another person to that risk. I felt, if I believed so much in the purpose of the surgery — its importance and the science behind it — that I should take that risk. But to me, it was a calculated risk. Just like the justices, Dr. Julipo had my consciousness stored in case the upload failed."

"What does it feel like? To be inside a robot?" asked Goggins.

Dr. Redford let out a laugh. It sounded like mine. A bit of a grunt. Both Zara and Goggins shook their heads at me.

"Pardon my laugh. It's a bit rough, but it's the best I can do," he said. "It feels like you're contained in a room at first. Like you're just observing. Soon after learning to control the robotic body parts, the legs, arms, and mastering walking, you graduate to utilizing the CPU to full capacity, having data at your finger-tips at a speed that is breathtaking. Then you feel a bit — euphoric."

"Invincible?" said Goggins.

"Different than that. You feel like you want to solve all the problems in the world. And then, after a few months, that subsides, and you can continue on in a more level-headed way," he said.

Dr. Redford turned to me. "Gabe, do you feel like that?"

"No, not at all," I said. "I've never felt euphoric."

"I'm not sure if the justices will feel that way. We will, of course, be monitoring them closely," said Dr. Redford.

The door of the lab opened, and two human medtechs escorted three robots into the room. It was the future supreme court justices — well, their robotic bodies, at this point.

"Thank you. Please stand over there," said Dr. Redford, pointing to the back of the room.

The robots stood where directed in a row and lined up obedi-ently. The medtechs left the room.

The robots were of the same grade and model as Dr. Redford. They were black in color, with the same build that we shared.

We all went over to inspect them.

"They look wonderful, Doctor," said. Dr. Julipo.

"Yes, I'm quite happy with them," said Dr. Redford.

"So, they take direction from you specifically?" asked Goggins.

"Yes, until the surgery. Then they will be autonomous and will only take direction internally from the justices," said Dr. Redford.

"Do you mind if we review their code? To familiarize ourselves with it before the surgery tomorrow?" asked Zara.

"Certainly. I mean, what you can find, you're free to peruse, but some of the code is encrypted for security and proprietary reasons. All the code is also locked and can't be tampered with.

After all, Ameribot Industries did win the contract," said Dr. Redford.

"Yes, we understand," said Goggins. "I assume they will make trillions if all goes according to plan."

"Most likely," said Dr. Redford.

"And you become infamous," said Zara.

"I suppose. Along with Dr. Julipo. But that's not why I'm doing this. And I don't mean to speak for you, Doctor. But we must preserve the lives of these three justices."

"At least that is what Ameribot proposed, correct?" I asked.

"Um, yes. Ameribot began the conversation with a study," said Dr. Redford. "But the justices were very open to the idea."

"They were?" asked Zara.

"Yes, I was surprised too," said Dr. Julipo. "At the first meeting, they didn't seem interested, but then we had a second meeting, and they were all in." He laughed with enthusiasm.

I thought for a moment. First meeting, they opposed the idea and the second meeting, they were *all in.*

"What do you suppose changed their minds?" I asked.

"I don't know exactly. They must have agreed with the Galactic Council's choice of Ameribot Industries winning the contract and heard the answers they needed to feel comfortable with the surgery," said Dr. Julipo.

Interesting.

Goggins and Zara began to examine the robots. Their eyes were closed. "Where are their activation buttons?" asked Goggins.

"They don't have any. They have a renewable energy source," said Dr. Redford.

Goggins shot a glance at me. "They look like they're in hibernation."

"If you directly address them, they will awaken. Just ask them a question."

Goggins stood in front of one of the robots. "Robot, what is your name?"

The robot's eyes opened. "I don't have a personification name yet, but I will soon, after the procedure with the Supreme Court justice. I'm SJC-3 Supreme Judge Bot C Series number 3. You may call me Three until the procedure is completed. That will be the next sol."

"Thank you, Three," said Goggins.

"You may call this robot to my left One. And to my right is Two," said Three. Each robot opened its eyes when their number was called out.

They were sentient. And they already had a consciousness, whether humans wanted to acknowledge that or not. And I didn't know how the robots' consciousnesses would interact with or acquiesce to the justices' consciousnesses. Obviously, Dr. Redford had worked this out but *how* is what I wanted to know.

"Their renewable battery is supported by what source?" asked Zara.

"It has —" started Dr. Redford, but he was interrupted by Three.

"Allow me, Dr. Redford."

"Certainly, Three."

"All of us have a battery that is powered by a crystal and placed in our chest. It is called Bakulite," said Three.

"I'm familiar with it," said Zara.

"Dr. Redford has invented a way to harness its energy, safely, I may add, within our armor. He has it also," said Three.

"Bakulite has only been used in starships," said Goggins.

"Yes, but I was able to extract a smaller amount for robots," said Dr. Redford.

"You have found a way to have the robot defer to a human's consciousness," I said. "I mean, if you believe robots have a consciousness."

"I can't say if they do. I never sensed one once my operation was complete. All I know is my human consciousness is full and intact."

"What happened to your robot's personality?" asked Zara.

Dr. Redford laughed. "It simply went away."

Somehow, I didn't believe it was that simple.

"Dr. Redford, one more question."

"Yes, Gabe?"

"Where is the first person who survived the surgery?"

"That robot, I mean, person, is now embedded with the Heragi military. I believe they are assigned to a General Foxwell," said Dr. Redford.

Goggins pushed his fingers through his hair, and Zara shook her head. Neither said a word but we all felt the same way, I was sure.

Foxwell. Great. Not.

7

———

The next sol, we arrived with Dr. Julipo at the medbay and were ushered into the decontamination room to prepare for the surgeries. A sterilization light came on and removed any possible infection particles on their bodies or my armor.

Dr. Redford was already present, with the three robots. They sat in the middle of the surgical room near an array of computers and monitors. There were three surgical tables in the middle where each justice would be operated on, one at a time.

Goggins and Zara had reviewed the code in the robots yesterday evening. The prime directive on all three robots was identical.

To support and defend the Zephon Galactic Council's constitution against all enemies with faith and allegiance.

They were both impressed with the coding and the CPU unit Dr. Redford designed. It was fast, and the number of galactic legal cases it held from the past few thousand years, condensed on a small directory, was staggering.

They found nothing irregular. Which, to me, was highly irregular, knowing Ameribot Industries.

Dr. Julipo would be performing the brain surgery on the

justices to extract all brain cells that would be digitally duplicated and then transferred to two places. The first location would be a computer that would run the electric impulses from the brain cells into a drive to be inserted into the robot.

The second location transferred the brain cells to a protoplasm mass that would be sphere-like when formed. The spheres would be self-encased and float in a glass filled with hydrogen.

There would be three floating spheres, the Supreme Court justices' consciousnesses, in the large glass cylinder when the surgeries were completed and kept as backups if anything went wrong with the robots. And later, the Supreme Court justices could give permission for them to be destroyed.

When I inquired yesterday if the doctors believed that a person's consciousness was wholly stored in their memory cells, they both said no. When I asked where it does exist and how they could transplant it from a human to a robot, they explained they thought it was in the pineal gland. And that they were able to decipher pulses in its cells that translated to what they believed was the essence of a person's consciousness.

Yesterday, when I asked if this consciousness was the soul of a person, Dr. Redford didn't reply; he shrugged his shoulders and busied himself on a nearby computer.

But Dr. Julipo stepped closer to me and said, "I don't know. I don't think so. I think it's something more that we will never be able to truly capture."

"Do you believe I have a soul?" I asked him.

Dr. Julipo stared deep into my eyes. "Yes, I believe so."

"Where did it come from?" I asked.

"I believe a part of it somehow comes from your creators. Don't tell me how I know that, just that it makes the most sense for me. At least that is what I want to believe."

"And my consciousness?" I asked.

"You think, don't you?" he asked.

"Yes, of course,"

"Then you have a consciousness." And then he touched my arm and sauntered away.

I sat up the whole night while Goggins and Zara slept in Deter's apartment and thought of what Dr. Julipo said. I may have a part of Ava and Damiel inside of me. Part of their souls. My chest hurt and then was warmed when I thought of them. I hoped that it was true.

Dr. Julipo and Dr. Redford discussed a few items ahead of time and then motioned to some medtechs to bring in the justices.

Zara and Goggins were stationed at a computer where they would be reviewing the coding transfer from the justices to the robots. I would be stationed near them.

The medtechs first brought in Guy, then Tefara and then Lilou. Their heads were shaven and they were still conscious.

Dr. Julipo gave them each an anesthetic shot. I watched Guy and Tefara close their eyes, and they were then in a coma. I gazed down at Lilou. She locked onto my eyes and then she spoke in my mind. *Gabe, if I do not awaken, I want you to know it was a pleasure knowing you.*

I moved toward her and stopped. She smiled and closed her eyes.

I couldn't say anything to anyone at the moment. I just thought back to her, *The pleasure was mine.*

Did anyone in the surgical room know Lilou was telepathic? Did anyone in the galaxy know she was telepathic?

She was an Oliverian. I wasn't aware her species had the ancient gifts. I would have to do more research on this after the surgery. I wondered if she had shared her gift with the other justices. Or if she had ever used her telepathic gifts while in the courtroom on a case.

I had to clear my head and think of the matter at hand — the surgery.

I stepped back and watched as Dr. Julipo opened the skulls of the justices and hooked wires to them that would essentially code the cells and pulses emanating from those brilliant minds.

Dr. Redford monitored the glass cylinder where three floating spheres emerged. Each sphere pulsated and changed colors as they floated. I was mesmerized watching them. I wondered which one was Lilou.

Dr. Redford peered over the shoulders of Goggins and Zara. They were reviewing the code transfers to the robots' CPUs. Each robot was becoming one of the justices before our eyes.

The first robot that received code was Guy.

The second robot was Tefara.

And the last robot to receive code was Lilou.

Goggins turned to Dr. Redford. "How will we know which one is which? Will they have the same voice? The robots here are identical in their body formations."

"Their voices will sound similar although not a perfect match to their human voices. They each will have a different eye color as they do in their human bodies."

"The code transfer is complete," said Zara.

"Excellent," said Dr. Julipo. "Any complications?"

"None that I can detect," said Zara.

"It all looks perfect," said Dr. Redford as he reviewed the monitors and then inspected each robot.

I scanned the three robots. Their eyes were opening. Code flashed before their eyes just like when Honora Kell received my code.

Guy opened his eyes, and they were brown.

Tefara opened her eyes, and they were green.

Lilou opened her eyes, and they were blue.

The three justices' human bodies were still. Their bio-metrics went silent and were presumed un-alive.

Dr. Julipo and Dr. Redford shook hands.

"Take the justices' human bodies away please," ordered Dr.

Julipo. The medtechs wheeled the three bodies out of surgery. My chest hurt.

We all surrounded the robot-justices.

Dr. Redford went to the end of the tables. "Justice Guy Cadiux, please sit up." The robot with brown eyes didn't move. Then we saw its legs very slightly tremor. Then it spoke. "How? How do I do that, exactly?" he asked with a slight stutter. Guy was making connections now with his pre-programmed robotic CPU and his human brain cells. His voice was not an exact duplicate of Guy Cadiux's voice but very similar.

"You need to practice and imagine making the movement. The neurons in your brain need to make a connection to your body sensors. Try," said Dr. Redford.

"I am," said Guy. There was no detectable stutter. I was impressed that Guy's speech could be so smooth.

We watched as his legs trembled again. He grunted. It was remarkable to witness this renaissance.

Then Guy raised himself at the waist. He was sitting up. "I did it," he said with a bit of excitement.

"Excellent," said Dr. Redford.

Guy glanced around the room. "Amazing." He turned to his colleagues. "Did they make it?"

"Yes, we're just about to wake them. You were the first," said Dr. Redford.

"How do you feel?" asked Dr. Julipo.

Guy grunted again. "That's my laugh? It sounds awful." He tilted his head slightly toward Dr. Redford.

"Yes, but we're used to it," said Goggins, looking at me.

"I feel — different." He brought up his arm and twisted it around. "I feel new."

"Yes, in a manner, you are," said Dr. Julipo. "Time to wake the others."

Dr. Redford turned to Tefara Kimathi. He went through the same procedure. After a few tries, Tefara was sitting up and looking at all of us. "Is that what I look like?" She pointed at Guy.

We all laughed. "Yes, but you have your green eyes," said Dr. Julipo.

"Good," said Tefara. "I remember you telling us that. I don't want to be mistaken for Guy."

Guy grunted. "They said our laughter will get better."

"No, it doesn't get better. But you'll get used to it," said Goggins with a chuckle.

"If that is all I have to get used to for the price of immortality, then it is worth it," said Guy.

"Indeed," seconded Tefara.

"Go on, Dr. Redford," said Dr. Julipo.

"Justice Lilou Prado, please rise."

The robot with the blue eyes rose without a struggle. Lilou moved her head and turned to her fellow justices. "I'm so glad we all made it. Congratulations, doctors."

"Congratulations to you, Justice Prado. How do you feel?"

Lilou moved her arms and stared at her hands. "Like I want to run and jump as if I were a child."

"Yes, yes. And you will. We will have physical therapy sessions for the next few days as you all learn to control your new bodies," said Dr. Julipo.

Lilou glanced at me. She sent me a thought. *I made it.*

I sent her back a thought. *How in the galaxy did you know that I could hear you?*

I heard about you.

From Anjori?

Yes.

Have you always been telepathic?

Yes.

I didn't know Oliverians possessed the ancient gifts.

They don't. I'm only three-quarters Oliverian. My grand-mother was Heragian and had the gift.

That is not in your personal record.

No, it is not.

Dr. Redford asked the justices to stand and follow him to a back room where they would begin their acclimation process. The three justices were a bit wobbly on their feet but were able to slowly walk to the door.

"Could Gabe attend also?" asked Lilou as she turned around.

"Um, Gabe?" said Dr. Redford, surprised by the request.

"I'd be honored. I'll be right there," I said.

The justices left the room with Dr. Redford.

Dr. Julipo turned to us. "Did you observe anything that worries you?"

"I didn't. The operation was fascinating. Dr. Redford is brilliant, as you said beforehand," said Zara.

"Nothing was apparent. But I would suggest we keep monitoring. We're here for a few more days and can assist with that," said Goggins.

I studied the justices' three floating consciousness spheres. I wondered if they would now be diverging since the duplicate consciousnesses were in different entities and experiencing different sensations and actions.

"Gabe? What do you think?" asked Dr. Julipo.

"I think Dr. Goggins is right. We need to keep monitoring. This is too important to say that all is well," I said.

"Okay then. I will defer to your experiences. Thank you for assisting. But please keep an open mind. Ameribot's work on this may be coming from a legitimate and compassionate place." Dr. Julipo left the room.

I turned to Zara and Goggins. "I have something to tell you."

"What?" asked Zara.

"I didn't want to say this in front of the doctors for obvious reasons. But Lilou is telepathic."

"What?" Goggins ran his hands through his hair.

"She's Oliverian," said Zara.

"And part Heragi," I said. "She sent me thoughts right before the surgery and right afterward. She retained the gift."

"I'll be fizzled," said Goggins.

"What does this mean?" asked Zara.

"I don't know," I said.

"She obviously feels comfortable enough with you to share that information," said Goggins. "Hey, how did she know you could reply back?"

"Anjori," I said.

"Another question is why she shared this information with you," said Zara.

"She must have been afraid to lose the ability after the operation," said Goggins.

"Yes, perhaps," I said.

"Either way, she's reaching out to you," said Zara. "For something. Don't take that lightly."

I nodded and headed out of the room. "I'll meet you back at the apartment," I said, heading to the physical therapy room. Justice Lilou Prado must want something from me, I just didn't know what it was at this point.

8

In the physical therapy room, Dr. Redford had the justices continue their neuron synapsis exercises to control their new robotic bodies. They underwent calisthenic and agility moves that at first bewildered them but after repetition, they found joy in performing.

It was good to hear the justices laugh, even if it was the grunt that I shared with them, as they mastered their new bodies. Although they also couldn't smile, I could see delight in their head tilts and how they encouraged each other.

My chest warmed. I felt close to them.

As I helped them grasp objects and even throw and catch, they would ask me and Dr. Redford questions. They were as curious as children, at least from my limited experience with the Kell children.

Tefara missed catching a heavy ball Guy tossed to her, and it hit her leg. She didn't flinch. She just picked it up.

"That didn't hurt?" I asked.

"No," said Tefara. "Is it supposed to?"

"Not at all," said Dr. Redford. "You won't feel any pain."

"Externally," I said.

"No pain," said Dr. Redford, a bit annoyed. I think he resented me assisting him outside of the operating room. If it weren't for Lilou asking me to help, I wouldn't be in this room.

"Do you feel pain, Gabe?" asked Guy.

I decided to answer truthfully. "Yes, I do."

"Why did your creators do that?" asked Lilou.

"They wanted me to be empathetic to non-robots," I explained.

"Why would that be needed? Your prime directives keep humans safe," said Dr. Redford.

"Yes, that is true." I had to lie.

"Curious," said Dr. Redford.

"Gabe, can you help me over here?" asked Lilou. I crossed the room and helped her work on finger dexterity as she handled her comm device.

"You seem to be progressing," I said to her quietly.

"Yes, I'm happy the operation was a success rather than having my consciousness floating around in a glass bottle."

I chuckled. "Yes, agreed."

She sent me a thought. *Were you surprised when I sent you a thought before the surgery?*

I'm still surprised.

Do you trust Dr. Redford?

From what I have heard and seen, he's been truthful. But I want to keep monitoring you and the other justices before we leave.

And when is that?

Soon. I have a friend who is awaiting trial.

What's your friend's name?

Stoller.

I watched as Lilou closed her eyes. When she opened them, code was crossing over her eyes.

What are you accessing?

The Justice Station's court directory, she thought back to me.

She was bringing up Stoller's case.

I see his lawyer is Deter Finz.

Yes.

He has two witnesses arriving tomorrow.

I nodded.

Jessio Rothworth?

Yes.

If Deter is good — and I believe he is — then he has a good chance of having the charges dismissed.

Thank you for that free legal advice.

You're welcome.

Dr. Redford headed over to us. I spoke aloud to Lilou. "That's it. Keep working your fingers."

"Ah, yes, thank you Gabe," she said.

Dr. Redford peered over her comm device. "Very good, Lilou." He backed up to speak to the justices. "You have all done wonderful for your first day. I need to file an update with the Galactic Council. Please feel free to retire to your quarters."

"Thank you, Dr. Redford. May we walk around the station?" asked Guy.

He wasn't comfortable with this question. "I have to complete my report."

"Gabe can escort us around," offered Lilou.

"We won't get into any trouble," said Guy with a grunt.

"No one will even recognize us," said Tefara.

He couldn't refuse them. They were, after all, Supreme Court justices, and I would be with them with a concealed gun hidden in my back. Although Redford didn't know about the gun.

"Yes, certainly. You are all free to walk around the station. You're not prisoners," said Redford, and he walked out of the room.

All the justices gathered around me.

"Where should we go?" asked Tefara with excitement in her voice.

"The observatory deck," said Guy.

"Yes, anywhere sounds better than this room. I'm tired of being in medbay," said Lilou.

"Okay, the observatory deck it is," I said as I turned for the door.

We left the medbay and merged into the crowd of bustling commuters. The justices ran into a few people as their bodily reactions weren't quite up to speed yet.

"Ooof," said Guy as he took a hard hit from an oncoming alien on the way to a courtroom that spun him around in a circle.

"Careful," I said, trying to shelter them from the passing Justice Station employees, residents and visitors. "Dr. Redford will be very upset if you get hurt."

"Isn't that practically impossible?" said Tefara.

"Yes. Not feeling pain may seem like an advantage, but sometimes it helps to know what your limits are," I said. Geez, I felt like I was parenting.

"I feel limitless," said Guy. He bounded up an escalator.

"Guy!" I yelled. Yep, definitely parenting. "Careful!"

Before I knew it, Tefara was running up the stairs after him. And then Lilou turned toward me. I shrugged my shoulders and said, "Go ahead. I know you want to."

"Thanks," she said as she ran after her colleagues. I could hear grunt laughter as she ran up the escalator. I ran after them.

They were all a bit wobbly as they first began running, but with each level, their agility improved.

We reached the top level for the observatory on the second hub. They slapped each other's backs in congratulations.

"I feel like a kid," said Guy.

"That was incredible," said Tefara. "Gabe, what else can we do?"

"Practically anything," I said.

Tefara did a handspring. She bounced into a plant stand, nearly knocking it over. "Whoa."

Lilou laughed, enjoying the show of her colleagues.

"Redford is going to kill me," I joked.

"We'll defend you," said Guy. He jumped up and balanced on a railing.

"Whoa. I think you should come down," I said, looking around. People were starting to stare. "You don't want to give robots a bad name, do you?"

He jumped down. "Sorry, Gabe. I don't. I just feel so much energy."

"Let's just enjoy the view for a minute," I said, trying to distract them. We watched a maintenance crew work outside in space on one of the wings of the station. There were robots working alongside humans and aliens in spacesuits, drilling and welding.

Tefara waved at one of the aliens in a spacesuit. It waved back.

"I have an idea," said Lilou.

"What?" asked Tefara.

"Let's take a walk outside the station," said Lilou.

"Outside. As in space?" asked Guy.

"I don't know, Lilou," said Tefara.

"Our feet have magnetic grips, don't they Gabe?" asked Lilou.

"Yes, all robots have them," I said. "But I don't think this is a good idea. You're just getting used to your new bodies."

Lilou gazed into a different direction. "There's a service gate down there." She pointed to a hallway with a tunnel. She was right.

This was like herding cicichimps.

Lilou took off with Guy and Tefara following her.

"Wait, wait," I yelled.

Then they started to run. I heard their grunting laughs all the way to the airlock chamber.

"You are Supreme Court justices." I ran after them, hoping a healthy dose of guilt would stop them.

"We're also human. We've been saddled with sickness and disease for years," said Lilou.

"Your operation was very expensive. What if the Galactic Council found out about this? They would think you went mad," I implored.

"They won't find out if we don't tell them. Come on, just a quick walk," said Lilou.

"Nothing is quick in space," I said. "Especially walking."

Lilou strode into the airlock chamber. Then Guy and then Tefara. They left me no choice. I walked in with them and closed the airlock chamber door and showed them how to turn on their gravity boots.

I depressurized the room, and their arms floated up, but their boots held them to the floor. They were delighted with the sensation.

"Are you sure you want to do this?" I asked. They all nodded. I shook my head. "This will be a short walk, understand?" They high-fived each other. It was never good to see humans doing high-fives unless it was at the end of a battle with the Heragi Empire.

"Here's a comm link. We'll be able to hear each other speak through this. Let's test it out first. It will be like I'm talking directly in your ear." I threw them the link in a hologram.

They each checked their arm comms.

"Can you hear me?" I asked. They all nodded. "Now when you speak in space, it will only be directed into our comm link."

They each touched their ear.

"Yes, that's amazing," said Guy.

"Yes," said Tefara.

"I can hear you, too," said Lilou.

"Okay, good." I opened up the hatch door and hooked them all to a tether, so no one would float away. That was all we needed was a rescue mission to save a Supreme Court justice. I would be booted off this station as soon as I got back inside.

For a minute, all they did was look out the hatch door.

"Spectacular," said Tefara.

"Now, everyone, follow me. Step carefully," I instructed.

Lilou followed me first, followed by Tefara and then Guy.

We proceeded forward out on the service ramp, and I led them over where there were no workers. We ventured onward out to the middle of the hub. I turned my head back. They were mastering the art of walking in space with their mag boots.

Guy let out a whoop. It was hard for me to remember these were Supreme Court justices, each over two hundred years old.

"Hey, watch this," said Guy. He did a little dance step. Tefara joined in and then Lilou. They resembled a robot chorus line step kicking to music. Utterly ridiculous and wonderful.

Tefara glanced at the stars all around the station. "How lovely it is out here. I could stay outside forever."

Guy wandered off as far as the safety cord would let him. He stared at a nearby planet with six moons.

Lilou approached me.

"Yes, Lilou?"

She shook her head and pointed to her temple. *I want to talk with you privately,* she thought to me.

I gazed into her blue eyes. *Yes?*

I'm sorry I forced your hand to take us out here.

It's okay. As long as Dr. Redford doesn't find out.

You have no idea how this feels. Or do you?

I haven't had much time for fun.

She nodded and looked over to her colleagues enjoying themselves. *Maybe you should,* she thought.

Yes, maybe I should, but there's been pressing matters.

Let me guess — the Heragi Empire?

You're aware of what they've been doing around the galaxy and to their own people.

Supreme Court justices don't live in a bubble. Yes, I know.

Can't you do something to stop it?

The law is only good when the citizens of the galaxy decide to utilize it. No one has brought a case to our court. It really is up to the Galactic Council to keep tabs on Heragi.

But they gave your robotic contract to them.

The justices and I discussed it. We decided to take the risk. If Heragi did indeed corrupt Ameribot Industries, then we will help expose it.

That's a big risk.

You will help us if something goes wrong.

I can't stay here forever, Lilou. I have a crew. Goggins, Zara and others who are depending on me.

For what?

For whatever comes our way as we fight for the freedom of the galaxy. I've seen what the Heragi military is up to, and it's not good for anyone in the chartered galaxy and the Edge.

She turned back to watch her colleagues.

This isn't going to end well, I fear, for you and the justices.

Take my hand.

What?

Take my hand. She reached out both her hands and I grasped them. She clicked off her magnetic boots and floated up into space, only being held to the station by me.

No, Lilou.

See, I trust you, she thought. *We all do.*

I pulled her in to me. I was holding her tight now. She clicked on her mag boots and secured herself to the station. I stared into her eyes. *Don't do that again.*

I won't. I promise.

You need to be careful.

I will.

I pushed her back a step.

Why are you sad?

You'll see, I thought, turning around and leading her back to the other justices. "Time to go back," I announced to all of them. None of them complained or asked for more time. They knew that I meant it was time to go. We headed back into the airlock chamber, and I closed the door. They all kept looking out the door window. I pressurized the chamber, they turned off their magnetic boots and we exited down the hallway in silence.

The justices all lived on the top floor of the third tier of the station near the Supreme Court rooms most likely for security reasons. They each had their own apartment.

We first stopped at Tefara's apartment. She opened up her door with a wave of her hand. Redford had inserted a security chip for each one of them to gain access to their apartments and the Supreme Court rooms.

Tefara hesitated and didn't step into her apartment. She turned to us. "I know it sounds silly, but I don't want to be alone right now."

"It's not silly," said Lilou. "I feel the same way. Why don't you come to my apartment and spend the night?"

"Yes, thank you," agreed Tefara.

Lilou opened her apartment door, and we walked into the spacious room with a wonderful view of deep space. I took a seat in her living room.

"Guy, do you want to join us?" asked Lilou.

"Now that you mention it," said Guy. "I guess there's no harm in bunking with the girls. Gee, are we still he or she?" They all laughed.

"Gabe, what do you think?" asked Tefara.

"Your consciousnesses were female and for Guy, male. So, it reasons that you will still identify in that same way," I said. "But this is new territory for humans. Dr. Redford may be a good reference for you."

"Yes, he's been going through all of this alone," said Tefara.

"There is another," I said.

"Really? And where is that entity?" asked Guy.

"With the Heragi military," I said.

"In what capacity?" he asked.

"I'm not sure. But the uses are probably limitless when it comes to the technology to have a human consciousness in a robot," I said.

"We could be weaponized, couldn't we?" asked Tefara.

"Yes," I said. "That's why you need to let me, Goggins or Zara know if you believe anything doesn't feel right or if you perceive something wrong with each other."

They all nodded.

"Gosh, I wish I could have a drink. A nice whiskey. I think I will miss that. Eating and drinking," said Guy. "Amongst other things, but I haven't done that for years."

They all laughed heartily. I knew what they were talking about. It was funny. I just never thought about it. I never had a before and after as they had, being human or biological.

"And with that, I will let you all rest." I rose to leave.

"But we don't rest," said Guy.

"You're right," I said.

"So, what exactly should we do all night long?" asked Tefara.

"What do you do?" asked Lilou.

"After my humans go to sleep, I keep busy reading, reviewing my ship's logs and doing maintenance."

"And that fills up the hours?" asked Guy.

"You'll have to find your passion or a mission," I said.

"We have the law, our cases. We can do all of our writing and researching at night," said Tefara.

"Agreed. But with the speed of our CPUs, that could take an hour or two, tops." Guy let out a sigh.

"You'll have to find your way." I wished I could help more.

"Thank you, Gabe. It will be an adjustment, but we'll figure it out," said Lilou.

I nodded and left the apartment. My legs stopped halfway down the hallway. Then I turned around, headed back and knocked on Lilou's door. It automatically opened, and I entered back into the apartment to see the justices sitting in the living room. "I can teach you how to play a game that can take up hours and hours," I said.

"That would be wonderful," Guy said with excitement in his voice.

"Yes, it's called quinker. Ever hear of it?"

They all shook their heads no.

"Okay, gather around," I said.

And that is how I spent the first night with the galactic Supreme Court justices who had just become robots.

9

———————

The bailiff called for everyone in the courtroom to rise as Judge Ronni entered. Goggins, Zara and I stood up. I took a look at Stoller, who was conferring with Deter. His hair was tossed, and his overall appearance was unkempt. I was sure being gin-less for the past night was rough for Stoller.

Jessio Rothworth sat at the plaintiff's table. He wore a bright blue suit with his Rothworth family crest on it, which was a floating hologram of a red mountain. He smiled and waved at Stoller, who didn't wave back.

Zara nudged my arm and pointed to the witnesses Deter was able to track down and get transported from Charbeaux Station, and specifically the Blue Edger bar.

"That's Stoller's pilot-friend, Fargo," she said, pointing to an alien female dressed in an orange jumpsuit. I scanned her facial features. My alien directory brought up a match for the Pwebby species from the planet Pwebu. Her face had a crown of horns with moss growing on them that she picked at while she waited to be called up.

"I hope she doesn't pick her horns when she is called up to the stand," grimaced Goggins.

Zara pointed to the human sitting next to Fargo. "And that's Holin. He's the gold hunter." Holin was blond, and when he turned to smile at a Stoller, I saw a flash of gold. In fact, all his teeth were capped with gold.

"Blazes, he's going to blind the judge with those shiny teeth," cracked Goggins.

Maybe they were smarter than they looked. I hoped so.

"May all the witnesses please enter the box," said Judge Ronni as it pointed to a square, enclosed glass chamber.

The bailiff called out the witnesses. "Anno Fargo, Bus Holin and Jessio Rothworth, this way. The bailiff opened the glass chamber, and all three entered and took a seat. The bailiff pushed three white holographic halos over their heads where they hovered and glowed. Fargo and Holin had obviously never been to court because they ducked their heads thinking the halos would hurt them.

We could hear their voices as they spoke in the witness chamber.

"Whoa, what the heck?" said Fargo.

"It's just a witness halo," said the bailiff. "It will calculate the truthfulness of your statement."

"What?" said Holin.

"Just tell the truth," said Jessio as he smiled.

"Shove it. You know this is totally bogus putting Stoller on trial," said Fargo.

"You just stink at quinker," said Holin.

"Quiet," said Judge Ronni, pounding its gavel. They all shut up.

The court gallery laughed, as did Stoller, who might have thought the court gallery was somehow his friends, but they were all strangers.

"Counselor Finz. You are up first," said Judge Ronni. "Witnesses, please keep your answers succinct."

"What?" said Fargo.

"Short," said Judge Ronni.

I leaned over and whispered to Zara, "How does this work?"

"It's speed court. They have two minutes to interview all witnesses," said Zara.

"Why?" I asked.

"They data crunched all the past few hundred years of legal cases, and they found that elongated cases did nothing for the ultimate outcome. The faster the better," said Zara.

"And considering how many galaxy cases there are, this is the only way to keep up with them," added Goggins.

Judge Ronni rang a bell, and a blue neon hologram time counter appeared near the witness chamber that gave Deter two minutes of questioning. Deter ran up to the glass chamber and began his speed questioning. "Fargo, did you witness Jessio Rothworth lose a card game on the Charbeaux Station where James Stoller won Jessio's spaceship, the *Ravena*?"

"Yes, I did," said Fargo. The halo over her head turned neon green and then went back to white. "You see —" she continued before she was cut off by Deter who asked another question.

"Holin, did you also witness the same occurrence?"

"Yes, I did. Jessio is just terrible —" said Holin. His halo turned green, and he was cut off by Deter.

"And Jessio Rothworth, did you put up your spaceship, the *Ravena*, in the quinker pot that you lost to James Stoller?" asked Deter.

Jessio took his time and just stared at Deter.

"Mr. Rothworth?"

"Yes, I did." Jessio's halo turned green.

Deter smoothed the feathers on top of his head. "I rest my case. And ask your honor to move to dismiss this case." He breathed a sigh of relief. His witness time counter still had fifteen seconds left.

Judge Ronni stared at the witnesses and then spoke. "Mr. Rothworth, you made all these witnesses travel to the Justice

Station only for you to admit that you lost your ship in a card game?"

"Yes, your honor," said Jessio. His halo turned green.

"And will you enlighten the court on why you would do that?"

"Yes, your honor. Because James Stoller cheated in the card game. And that is how I lost the game." The halo glowed green again.

Stoller yelled, "I did not, you sore loser."

Judge Ronni tapped his hologram gavel. Deter quietly sauntered over and shoved his elbow into Stoller's rib cage.

"Sorry, Judge." Stoller tried to suck in air from Deter's jab. He wasn't sorry. If there was one thing that got under Stoller's collar, it was being accused of cheating.

"Will the prosecuting attorney, Ms. Rei, like to interview the witnesses?" asked Judge Ronni.

"Yes, Judge Ronni. Thank you."

Rei was very small, barely two feet tall. She moved with the use of a hovercraft to elevate herself up to the glass chamber. My alien directory identified her features as in line with the Beewins. Her timer glowed and started ticking as Judge Ronni rang the bell.

"Mr. Jessio Rothworth, why do you believe Stoller cheated in cards?"

"His sole intention was to steal my ship," said Jessio, and his halo turned green.

"What?" yelled Stoller as he jumped up. "Why is his halo green?"

Deter pulled down on Stoller. "This is why I didn't put you on the witness stand."

"We rest our case, Judge," said Rei. She still had over a minute and a half left.

The judge observed Rei. Even though its robotic face features did not have movable parts, much like mine, I would guess the judge was as perplexed as we all were in the courtroom.

"This case isn't about whether Mr. Stoller cheated at a card game. It's concerning if he stole your starship. So, based on the witnesses' testimony, my final judgement is that Mr. Stoller is cleared of all charges." The judge pounded its gavel, and the case was over.

Stoller jumped up and shook Deter's hand.

Then the judge pounded its gavel again. "And Mr. Rothworth and his legal team are fined three hundred thousand galaxy credits for knowingly filing false charges." It pounded its gavel again.

What? I turned to Zara and Goggins, who both had their mouths gaping open in surprise.

I checked back toward Jessio Rothworth, who was staring at me. He then turned to the judge and nodded his head in acceptance. His lawyer, Rei, had no emotion. She hovered near Jessio as he left the witness chamber and talked with her in hushed tones.

Stoller's witnesses, Fargo and Holin, came rushing out of the witness chamber and shook hands with him. We walked up to congratulate Stoller and Deter.

"Sorry for dragging your butts all the way over here for a few minutes," said Stoller.

"It was worth it to see Rothworth get fined," said Fargo.

"Yeah, like he meant to lose," said Holin.

"Yes, it was curious. Perhaps he wanted to inconvenience everyone," said Deter.

"Or he was really wanting one of those bounty hunters to blow you away," said Fargo with a laugh as she hit Stoller on the arm.

Stoller eye-balled me. Fargo had a point but so did Holin. Maybe Stoller's friends weren't as dim as they portrayed themselves on the witness stand. Doubtful, but possible.

"Hey, let's go grab a drink before you take off," said Stoller to his buddies.

"Just one? I think you owe us a few," said Fargo as she and Holin headed out the door.

Stoller turned to Deter and shook his hand again. "Thank you, Counselor. I appreciate it."

"You're welcome. I hope we never have to meet under these circumstances again."

"Agreed," said Stoller. "Hey, you guys want to join us?"

"Sure," said Goggins. "We can get you up to speed on the justices."

As Stoller passed by Jessio, he couldn't help but stop to say something to the wealthy Rothworth. "Say, Jessio. What was that all about?"

Jessio smiled. "I just wanted to annoy you."

"I hope it was worth three hundred thousand galaxy credits."

"It was. It really was."

"Hey, want to have another quick game before you leave the station?"

"Really?" said Zara, who was standing behind them both.

Jessio and Stoller both laughed. The sweetest revenge for people like Stoller and Rothworth was at the card table.

"You got it."

"Great. I'll send you the meet-up location later tonight."

We left with Stoller and his friends.

"Are you crazy?" said Goggins. "I thought you would hate that guy. You were almost made into space dust by Kaleb Kron and those other bounty hunters."

We were out in the hustle of the hallway now.

"He's here for a reason," said Stoller.

"You think this was all calculated?" I asked.

"Knowing Jessio, yes."

We followed Stoller down the hallway. He led us to a bar that he had heard about from his cell mate in jail. Leave it to Stoller to find the most interesting bar on the Justice Station.

On the same level as the station's ship gates was a hole-in-the-wall pilot bar called A Cup of Justice. It was frequented by those visiting the station for their trials who needed a drink but also wanted to keep a low profile. The bar was packed with aliens, humanoids and a few bots guarding their clients. The alien serving drinks behind the bar had eight hands which seemed to be very handy, excuse the pun, for its jam-packed bar.

"Leave it to Stoller to find a pilot bar," said Zara as she settled into a booth.

Stoller was already two rounds deep with Fargo and Holin at the bar. After a few minutes, they shook hands, and Stoller's friends left the bar to take the last shuttle back to Charbeaux Station.

"You know the old saying, a beoblard can't change its spots," said Goggins, looking at Stoller.

"Have you ever seen a beoblard?" asked Zara.

"No, but I saw pictures when I was a small boy. Not a very pretty animal," said Goggins.

Zara rolled her eyes.

I must be getting used to pilot bars because I was starting to feel comfortable in them. I stared out a nearby window and saw starships come and go from the outside gates, and my mind went to the *Alyssia*. I needed to visit Feti back on the ship. I felt bad I hadn't been in touch.

Stoller slammed down a tray filled with gin shots.

"Here's to the best crew a pilot could have," said Stoller as he hoisted a shot glass to us.

"We're *your* crew?" said Zara.

"We're each other's crew," said Stoller with a touch of a slur. The gin was already working.

"I don't mind. It's nice to belong," said Goggins. "I was always last picked in the schoolyard teams."

"How come that doesn't surprise me?" Stoller stared at Goggins, who frowned. Then Stoller turned his attention to me. "Gabe, how are the justices? They had their surgery?"

"Yes, they are adjusting," I said.

"You didn't find anything strange in the code?"

Zara shook her head. "It was elegantly coded. I mean, the code was impeccable. I've seen Gabe's code, and the justices' code is just as good or better." She glanced at me. "No offense, Gabe."

"None taken."

"I take offense," said Goggins. "Although I only coded Gabe's navigation system."

"And their prime directive was intact and locked in. No hanky-panky," said Zara.

Jessio Rothworth entered the bar with his own guard-bot, who was scanning the clientele for any potential threats.

"Jessio is here," I said.

"Let the fun begin. Anyone need a spaceship?" said Stoller as he got up to greet Jessio. "Welcome. Have a seat."

"Thank you. You can wait at the door," he said to his guard-bot, who scanned all of us at the table before leaving to station itself at the bar door.

"This is Zara, Goggins, and this is Gabe," said Stoller.

Jessio nodded. "Nice to meet you all. I saw you in the courtroom."

"Yes, and we saw you lose in the courtroom," said Zara.

Jessio smiled at her brazenness.

"Be nice, Zara." Stoller took out a pack of quinker cards from his pocket and began shuffling.

"It's all right," said Jessio. "It was an epic failure, I admit. I should have listened to my lawyer."

"It's all meteors under the Karakova Highway. Let's move on."

"He could have gotten you killed," said Zara, not letting up.

"I apologize," said Jessio as he glanced over to Zara.

"Hey, are you apologizing to her or me?" Stoller feigned hurt feelings.

"I think her," said Jessio. "She scares me more."

"Yeah, I don't blame you," said Goggins. "And I've known her forever."

"My pride was hurt, what can I say?" said Jessio.

"Speaking of pride. Sounds like your pride must have gotten another hit a few months ago. We heard you lost out on the Supreme Court robot contract," said Zara.

"Are we going to play quinker or what?" asked an annoyed Stoller as he dealt out cards to everyone but me, of course, the robot that counts cards. That was all right. I liked to watch.

Stoller called up a hologram from his comm device that had galaxy credits tabulated for each of the card players.

"Ameribot Industries beat us out on that. Not sure where we went wrong on the bid. Our robots would have been outstanding. The Galactic Council made a bad choice," said Jessio.

"We saw the robots. They're pretty impressive," said Goggins.

"I pray to the ancient ones that there isn't rogue code in those bots. Or every court case in the galaxy will be influenced by the Heragi Empire," said Jessio as he picked up his cards and rearranged them in his hand.

Zara shot me and Goggins a glance as she picked up her cards. "What? You think that is a possibility?" As if she didn't suspect the same thing.

Stoller began the game by discarding a card. They began their first round.

"They're in bed together. Everyone knows that, except the Galactic Council," said Jessio.

"So, your sol system isn't friendly with the Heragi Empire?" I asked.

"No, they've tried for a century to invade our system. When they realized they couldn't win a battle against our navy, they tried bribery and even tried to start a small battle between two planets that are in our federation. Infantile. We told them to take their treaty and blast it out their engines," he said with a wink.

"Interesting," said Stoller as he won the first hand.

"Frazzle me," said Jessio as he took one of Stoller's gin shots. "I need to pay more attention and talk less."

"We were able to look at the code. It was clean," said Goggins.

"Maybe you're not good enough to hack their code," said Jessio as he discarded.

"I don't take offense to that," said Goggins. "But she will." He pointed at Zara, who laid down her cards and won the quick second hand.

"Ouch. Apologies. I seem to be saying that a lot to you," said Jessio.

"What would you know about hacking?" asked Zara.

"Didn't you tell them, Stoller?" asked Jessio.

"Nope." Stoller concentrated on which card to discard. He picked a card, then cussed when he laid it down.

Jessio picked up the card. "Thank you. I'm the lead scientist for Roth Robots. And that's not a vanity title."

"Here I thought you were just a pretty rich boy," said Zara, who won another round.

"Shrieking asteroids," said Stoller under his breath.

"This has to be the last round. I have dinner plans with the Supreme Court justices tonight," said Jessio.

"Okay, quadruple or nothing, gang," said Stoller as the hologram showed Zara had the most winnings so far.

"You do?" asked Goggins.

"Yes, our family has kept friendly with all the justices for over a hundred years. So that is another reason I was hurt we didn't get the contract. It would have been like operating on family," said Jessio.

"Maybe you can take a peek at their code," said Goggins.

"Maybe," said Jessio. "It sounds like we are on the same side about the Supreme Court justices."

"Hey, if the code is clean, there is no side," said Stoller. "Zara, Goggins, weren't you impressed with their doctor? What's his name — Dr. Redford?"

"Yes, he seems extremely brilliant," said Goggins.

"We can't be naive about this," said Jessio. "If I gain access to the code and find something's not right, will you help?"

Zara, Goggins, Stoller and I nodded at each other. We agreed.

"Good," said Jessio as he laid down his last card. "Come to dinner tonight at Lilou's apartment on the top floor. I will let her know I've invited you all."

"Copy that," said Zara.

Stoller was the last to play his hand. He shook his head as Jessio let out a small shout of joy as he won the last hand.

"Just have those galaxy credits delivered to my account."

"Of course," said Stoller as he took a swig of his last shot.

Jessio got up to leave. "It's nice to be on the same side for once, Stoller." He winked at us and strolled out of the bar with his guard-bot.

"Do you actually trust Jessio?" asked Goggins.

"It's not that I wouldn't trust him. If he finds evidence that Ameribot tampered with the code, then okay, let's help. I would never let a dumb card game get in the way of saving the galaxy," said Stoller as he began to shuffle his cards.

"Maybe we missed something in the code, Zara," said Goggins.

"Maybe. It's always good to have an extra set of eyes," said Zara.

"Okay, then. Here's to an extra set of eyes," said Goggins. He took a swig of his drink.

I noticed something. "I counted the cards. You could have won that last hand."

He smiled at me.

"So, you let him win?" asked Zara.

"Yeah, of course. I let you win, too," said Stoller.

"But we lost *my* galaxy credits since I'm covering all of our losses," said Zara.

"Think of it as chipping away at what you owe me," said Stoller.

"You wanted Jessio to feel good when he left this bar," I said.

"There's a time to win and a time to lose," said Stoller with a wink. "Let's get ready for dinner."

He put his cards in his pocket, Zara paid the tab, and we left the bar to prepare for our dinner with the Supreme Court justices, only they wouldn't eat. So I wasn't sure exactly what to expect from this dinner.

10

———————

After leaving the bar, I headed to the *Alyssia* and told the team I would meet them at Lilou's apartment for the dinner with the justices and Jessio. I wanted to check in on Feti and the ship but mostly on Feti.

I reached the holding gate for the *Alyssia* and turned on my arm comm to notify Feti. I didn't want to surprise it. "Feti?"

"Yes, Gabe?"

"I'm coming on board. Could you lower the ramp?"

"Affirmative. Is everything okay?"

"Yes, I just wanted to stop in to say hello and check some items on the ship."

The *Alyssia*'s ramp lowered.

"There you go, Gabe. Okay, copy that."

I headed toward the bridge. It felt good to be back on board. I sat in my commander seat and checked some supply units.

"Hello, Gabe."

"Hello, there," I said. "How are you, Feti?"

"I'm doing fine. I missed you. Are we leaving?"

"I missed you, too. No, we're not leaving just yet. We may have to be here a few more sols. What have you been up to?"

"I've been keeping up to date with the news. The Justice Station has an incredible selection of galactic news, and they televise their court procedures on the station. I watched over two hundred court cases over the past few days. It was very interesting. I learned a lot."

I chuckled. "Did you watch Stoller's case?"

"Why, yes, I did. I'm very happy that he won and did not have to be sent to jail or worse."

"Yes, the team was happy, too."

"It was odd that Jessio Rothworth tied up the courts with such a case," said Feti.

"Yes, we thought so, too."

"If he was going to spend just ten minutes in the courtroom, I'm not sure why he arrived with two navy ships," said Feti.

"He what?"

"Yes. His navy ships are just off the station. They come and go, as to not look menacing. I'm tracking them though. I thought you would want me to do that, Gabe.".

"Why yes, thank you. That is interesting."

"I thought so."

"Any other items you have found strange?"

"There's a small asteroid storm coming through this evening. Nothing terrible. All ships that are tucked into the station should be fine. I'll inform you if I find anything else."

I checked to see if we had our supplies replenished as I requested when we landed at the station. All supplies were filled.

A thought came to me. "So no pings or notifications from any of the Kells?"

"No. No messages or location pings. Are you expecting comms from them?"

"No," I said. "I just wondered."

"I miss them too."

Feti understood me better than I thought.

"How are the three justices doing after the surgery? It's been all over the news."

"They're adjusting."

"Hmm. I wish them well. I watched a few documentaries on them. They seemed like good humans. Actually, exceptional humans."

"Yes, I hope they continue to be good justices."

"I have to admit something to you, Gabe."

"What would that be?"

"I tracked you the other night. I noticed you were outside of the space station."

"Yes, that's true."

"With the three justices."

"Wow. You are good."

"Be careful, Gabe. They are very important robots."

"Yes, I will be," I said, a bit ashamed. "They need to get used to their new bodies and being robots. They're excited."

"Yes, I imagine that would happen. And they will have to handle the loneliness."

I stopped fidgeting with the console and sighed. Feti understood.

"That is what I'm worried about, amongst other things," I said.

"That is why you visited me, isn't it? You didn't want me to be lonely."

"Yes, that's true."

"Thank you."

"You're welcome," I said. "The justices will have to learn to cope."

"Yes, you can help them."

"I'll try."

And then we sat together for the next hour as we both kept ourselves busy reviewing the *Alyssia*'s maintenance check lists and chatting. It was nice. It felt good. After saying goodbye and promising to visit again the next sol, I went back to the main hub of the station. I hoped Feti was healthy for many years. We both needed the companionship. As would the justices.

We showed up outside of Lilou's apartment at the time that Jessio confirmed with us earlier for the dinner party. I rang the doorbell.

"How do I look?" asked Stoller. He had bought a new shirt. He actually cleaned up pretty well, if I'm a good judge of that.

"Like you're trying too hard," said Zara.

"Why the new shirt?" asked Goggins.

"Hey, these are Supreme Court justices. Never hurts to dress to impress," he said.

"Are you competing against Jessio?" asked Goggins.

"No."

"That's good because he's much better looking than you," said Zara.

The door opened, and Lilou was there wearing a colorful caftan over her robotic body. "Hello, please come in," she said.

Jessio sat on a couch talking with the other two justices. He toasted his drink to us. "Now the party can get started," he said.

"Indeed." Stoller put a bottle of wine on the table.

"How I wish I could enjoy that wine," said Guy. "Hello there, I don't think we've met." He reached out a hand to Stoller.

"This is James Stoller. James, this is Justice Guy, Tefara and Lilou," said Jessio.

"Pleasure to meet you," said Tefara.

"Thank you for the wine," said Lilou. "We're happy to entertain just as we did in the past."

We took a seat in Lilou's living room.

"Do you miss it? Eating and drinking?" asked Goggins.

"Yes, but only the social aspect of it," said Lilou.

"I miss it. Tasting coffee and wine," said Guy. "But the advantages we now have are worth it."

"Yes. For example, today I read over fourteen hundred court documents and wrote two hundred correspondences," said Tefara.

"You are making very productive use of your time," said Zara.

The doorbell rang, and Lilou went to answer it.

Dr. Julipo came in. "Hello, hello everyone. Thank you for the invite, Lilou."

Jessio's shoulders twitched forward. I ran a bio-metric scan of his body. His temperature and neuron levels were rising. He wasn't expecting Dr. Julipo at the dinner party.

"Hello, Jessio. Nice to see you," said Dr. Julipo.

"What a nice surprise. How are you? Congratulations on the successful operation," said Jessio.

"Thank you. Everything proceeded accordingly," said Dr. Julipo.

"And for that, we should toast." Stoller poured a glass of wine for all the humans. "Cheers."

"I want a glass," said Guy. "If only to toast." Stoller poured a glass for Guy and also for Tefara and Lilou and for me. We all raised our glasses and clinked them.

"Excellent," said Goggins as he took a swig.

A hologram popped up from Lilou's arm comm, signaling the meal was ready. Lilou stood up. "Let's move on to the dining room."

We followed Lilou into an elaborate dining setting and seated ourselves. The three justices went into the kitchen and each carried out a variety of gourmet dishes.

"It smells wonderful," said Jessio. "What a surprise. My home planet's specialties."

"Yes, to honor our friendship over the years," said Lilou. "Enjoy."

The humans passed around the dishes, and the justices seem to gather real pleasure from watching them enjoy the meal they prepared. I found it amusing, but since I never tasted food or wine, I didn't gain the same pleasure in observing humans eat.

"You are supreme chefs too," said Dr. Julipo.

"I never had time to cook in the past," said Tefara.

"But now we have all the time in the world." Guy touched his wine glass.

"So, no major adjustments have had to be made since the surgery?" asked Jessio.

"No, everything is working properly. Isn't that right, Dr. Julipo?" said Lilou.

"Yes, they are advancing rapidly with their dexterity," he said.

"Good. That's wonderful," said Jessio.

"Jessio, I know you must be disappointed that your company did not win the justices' robotic contract," said Dr. Julipo.

Jessio smiled. "Yes. I have to admit, it hurt a bit. Knowing the deep history that my family has had with all the justices."

"There will be more opportunities in the future on other projects, I'm sure," said Dr. Julipo.

"Yes, I'm sure. And for now, perhaps you and the justices will allow me to get a peek at some of the code."

"I don't know," said Dr. Julipo. "Dr. Redford said it is proprietary."

"Who exactly owns my code? Don't we own it?" asked Guy.

"Good question," asked Tefara. "Dr. Julipo?"

"I don't think this is Dr. Julipo's jurisdiction, if I may. No one can own our code besides us. It's a part of us now," said Lilou.

"Indeed," said Goggins as he drank another sip of wine.

"The Galactic Council will not want just anyone poking around in your code," said Dr. Julipo.

"Am I just anyone?" said Jessio.

"I don't mean it that way," said Dr. Julipo.

"How did you mean it? I may be one of the justices' true friends," said Jessio.

"True friends?" said Dr. Julipo.

"We agree and would like Jessio to review our code. Zara and Goggins didn't find any tampering of code by Ameribot Industries. But it doesn't mean it's not there."

The dining room was quiet. I glanced over to Dr. Julipo. I performed a bio-metric scan of his body. His nervous system levels were starting to rise.

"This isn't good. As much as I respect all of you, I feel that this could be treacherous to our friendship with Ameribot Industries," he explained.

"But how good a friend are they if they have corrupted the code?" asked Jessio.

"Speculation, speculation," said Dr. Julipo thrusting his hands into the air.

"Let us settle this," said Lilou as she stood up. "When you have finished dinner, we will go down to Dr. Julipo's lab. There, Jessio can review our code."

"Is that satisfactory to everyone?" asked Tefara.

Everyone agreed.

Lilou sent me a thought from across the table. *Do you trust Jessio?*

I do not trust or distrust him. We only met today. And you?

I have known him since he was a small boy. Yes.

Code is binary, as you know. That is where the truth lies.

Lilou nodded at me from across the table.

After dinner, the whole party went down to the medbay lab. Dr. Julipo turned on the lights and computers. The three justices sat in chairs, and Zara, Goggins and Jessio connected their coders to them. On the monitors, all three of the justices' directories and coding programs began to flash on the screen.

Dr. Julipo stayed by the door and leaned against a wall. He was not happy about this late-night code review. Stoller and I took seats to watch the scientists share their discoveries.

Lilou watched as her code flew by on the monitors. I couldn't begin to imagine what she and the other justices were feeling.

"Look, their prime directive looks fine." Zara pointed to the monitor for Jessio to review.

"Yes, it does," he said. He began searching their directories.

"What are you looking for?" asked Goggins.

"Any encryptions," he replied.

"Yes, Dr. Redford mentioned many files are encrypted," said Goggins.

Jessio began typing at lightning speed. "What's that?"

"What?" said Goggins as he studied the monitor closer along with Zara.

"It was behind that transponder code. Look," said Jessio.

Dr. Julipo scurried over. "What is it?" He squinted his eyes to see the code. "I never saw that before."

"It's hidden," said Jessio.

Then the lab door burst opened.

Dr. Redford marched in. "What's the meaning of this?" He pushed Jessio away from the monitors. Jessio flew to the floor.

"Dr. Redford," yelled Lilou.

"He's sabotaging your code," said Dr. Redford.

"Or perhaps we just found the bogus code you planted in the justices," said Jessio as he got up.

Stoller leaned over and whispered to me, "This could get ugly." We both stood up, ready to restrain or put down anyone who got too heated in the room.

"This code. It shouldn't be here," said Zara.

Dr. Redford went over and surveyed the code. "I didn't write that. He must have just implanted it."

"But you said you had a code freeze on it that essentially locked down any code changes," said Goggins.

"I don't know about you all, but I'm getting tired of people poking around in my code," said Guy as he pulled the connection wires out of his chest and stood up.

"We're just trying to make sure you're okay. All of you," said Jessio.

"I'm okay. Look." Guy pounded his arm down on a chair and shattered it. "I never felt more alive."

"Whoa, careful. We don't mean to upset you," said Dr. Julipo.

"Guy, come sit down," said Lilou.

"No, I'm tired of sitting." He pushed away a chair and left the room.

"Guy, stop," yelled Tefara as she ran after him.

"Look what you've done," yelled Dr. Redford.

"Dr. Julipo, call the Galactic Police. They need to arrest Dr. Redford for crimes against the justices and the Galactic Council. Ameribot has corrupted the justices' code," said Jessio.

"Hold on—" said Dr. Julipo.

"We need to get Guy and Tefara back here. They have rogue code in them," said Jessio.

Jessio ran to the wall comm and called the Justice Station police. "Help, we need help. Two Supreme Court justices are loose. We need to capture them. They have rogue code."

"What are you doing?" said Dr. Redford.

"We're not criminals," said Lilou. "I'm going after them." She ran after her colleagues.

"Stoller," I cried as I chased after Lilou.

Lilou was already gone from the hallway. She was fast. Stoller and I ran out into the main hub, into the crowd of Justice Station commuters. We turned to view each direction.

"Where are they?" asked Stoller.

"I think I know where Guy is headed," I said.

"Where?"

"Outside the station." I ran for the nearest escalator. I bounded up the stairs with Stoller doing his best to keep up. I saw a glimpse of Lilou. I yelled out her name. She glanced back at me but didn't stop.

Help, Gabe, she thought.

I'm trying.

I hit my arm comm to get a link to Zara and Goggins. "Get to the *Alyssia* and travel just out of the station. Get over to service exit twenty," I yelled.

"Copy that," said Zara.

"You got it, Gabe," said Goggins.

I hit my comm link again. "Feti?"

"Yes, Gabe?"

"Start your launch procedures. Zara and Goggins will be boarding."

"Copy that."

Stoller and I ran up the myriad of escalators to the top of the observatory. I could see Tefara and Lilou outside the service door airlock chamber. Inside the chamber was Guy. Stoller and I ran up to the door. The airlock chamber was locked.

"Open the door," I yelled

"Don't do this, Guy," pleaded Lilou.

Guy shook his head no.

He depressurized the chamber and opened the external door.

Then the Supreme Court justice floated out into space.

11

"No!" yelled Tefara as she pounded on the observatory deck window. We watched Guy float out into space.

The external service door closed.

"I'm going out there," I said to Stoller.

"I'm coming with you." He pressurized the airlock chamber and found an emergency spacesuit used by the station's service team.

"Feti told me earlier there's an asteroid storm coming in."

"Then we better be quick."

"How was Guy acclimating to his new life as a robot?" I asked Tefara and Lilou.

"Obviously, having a hard time," said Stoller as he put on his spacesuit.

"He was walking around the station a lot. He just couldn't sit still this past sol," said Tefara.

"How long can he survive out there?" asked Lilou.

"For many hours. I'm not so worried about that," I said.

"What are you worried about?" asked Lilou.

"Space junk, asteroids. Space isn't that safe," chimed in Stoller.

"Stoller," I said, trying to stop him from speaking.

"Sorry," said Stoller.

"Guy," whispered Tefara as she stared out the window.

"Don't worry. We'll retrieve him," I said.

"Thank you," said Lilou.

I entered the airlock chamber, and Stoller closed the internal door and depressurized the chamber. I stared into Lilou's blue eyes. I believed I could save Guy, but I wasn't positive. One never is positive when it comes to space. Stoller and I didn't bother locking down our magnetic boots, but instead, we fastened a safety line to both of us with me in lead position.

I hit my arm comm to establish a link to Stoller and the *Alyssia*. "Feti? Zara? Goggins?"

"Yes, Gabe," said Feti.

"We're here," said Zara.

"We copy you," said Goggins.

"Where are you?" I asked.

"Just pulling out of the station," said Feti.

"This is a rescue mission. Be prepared for a boarding through the external hatch door," I said.

"Copy that," said Feti. "Please be aware the asteroid storm is approaching."

"Copy that," I said. "But we're going anyway."

I nodded to Stoller, and he hit the opening to the external service door.

"There he is," I said, pointing. Guy was spinning in space. He was trying to right himself by extending his legs and twisting his body and pulling his legs back in. He was slowly stopping his spin.

"Ow, that would give me a headache," said Stoller.

"He wasn't built with any thrusters," I said.

"Are you?" asked Stoller.

"Yes. The Kells thought of everything," I said.

"Good thing," said Stoller.

We extended our arms, and with a soft touch, we pushed ourselves out of the Justice Station. Stoller and I used our thrusters to move steadily to Guy without having the same spin effect he had experienced leaving the airlock chamber.

"We have a visual on you, Gabe," said Goggins.

I turned my head and saw the *Alyssia* travel around the end of the station.

"Get me a comm to Guy," I said.

"Copy that," said Feti. "Gabe, the asteroid storm I mentioned to you earlier will be here in ten minutes. The risk assessment is high. You should abort your rescue mission to reduce casualties."

"Too late," I said.

Guy was able to control his spin. We were within a few hundred feet from him.

"Go ahead, Gabe. You have your comm link," said Feti.

"Thank you," I said. "Guy, can you hear me?"

I saw him hit the comm device on his arm.

"Go back, Gabe," said Guy.

"Not possible," I said.

"An asteroid storm is headed our way. And I don't think Dr. Redford made your armor strong enough to withstand a twenty-ton asteroid traveling at two hundred miles an hour," said Stoller.

"I just wanted some space, no pun intended. I feel so free out here," said Guy.

"When we approach you, don't move. I don't want you going farther out," I said.

"I didn't mean to jeopardize your lives," said Guy. 'I'm so sorry."

"We can talk about that later," said Stoller.

We were closing in and were now only fifty yards from Guy.

"Get ready for impact," I said.

"I have a visual on the asteroid storm," said Goggins.

"You need to move fast," said Zara.

"Trying," said Stoller.

Stoller and I reached out for Guy. We hit him harder than I wanted, and all three of us went spinning.

"Ooof," said Stoller. He had the worst of it being a human, and the spin was probably wreaking havoc on his brain. Stoller and I used our thrusters to stop our spin.

"Leave me, Gabe. I want to stay out here," said Guy.

The *Alyssia* moved in closer to us. Feti had opened its side door for us.

"Stoller, we need to detach from the station's line now," I said.

"Copy that," said Stoller as he let his line release. I detached mine.

Guy tried to push us off. I grabbed both of his arms to stop him from swinging.

"Stoller, you're going to have to steer us all to the *Alyssia*," I yelled.

"Move your butt, Stoller," yelled Zara.

An asteroid streamed past us two hundred yards away.

"That was too close for comfort," said Stoller as he pushed on his thrusters.

We were fifty yards from the *Alyssia*.

"Guy, stop it. I know it's hard. I know they didn't explain it all before you became a robot," I said to Guy. We were now face to face. I looked into his brown eyes.

"I can't go back," he said.

"To being human? No, you can't," I said.

Guy dropped his head and stopped fighting us. More asteroids flew. Stoller was getting us closer to the door. Forty yards, thirty yards — a large ice rock hit the *Alyssia*. Its door automatically closed with the impact. Stoller thrust us away from the *Alyssia* for safety.

"Ahhh," yelled Stoller.

The *Alyssia* spun. "We're hit," yelled Goggins.

"Get it under control, Feti," I called.

"Copy that, Gabe. Countering spin," said Feti. The *Alyssia* recharged its engines to counter the asteroid impact. Feti re-opened the door.

"Stoller, the door's open!" I yelled.

"Got it," said Stoller as he hit his thrusters. Rocks hurtled toward us. We were fifteen yards from the door. I turned backward and saw the storm of asteroids getting closer. We needed to get in immediately.

"Let me go. Save yourselves," said Guy has he tried to push away.

I slapped him across the face. "Sorry, Guy. You need to snap out of it," I said.

"Reaching—" yelled Stoller as he was able to grab the side of the open door. He yelled and, with one arm, pulled us all in. We hit the inside walls, and I let go of Guy. Stoller slammed the door valve, and it shut.

I hit the wall comm. "Feti, we're in."

"Hold on, Gabe," said Feti. The acceleration hit us hard, and we all slammed against the wall as Feti accelerated.

"Ahh," Guy yelled, not due to pain but surprise.

We moved around the other side of the station just in time as the asteroid storm passed.

"Pull yourself down to the ground," I ordered Guy. "Go ahead, Stoller." He pushed the valve to pressurize the airlock. We all steadied ourselves.

"That was close," said Stoller.

Guy crumbled to the ground. I kneeled and put my hand on his shoulder.

"I didn't mean to jeopardize you and your whole crew," he said.

"I know."

Stoller took off his helmet, "This? This was no big deal. We've been in hairy situations before." He walked away to give me and Guy privacy.

"I don't know if I can do this," he said. "Be a robot. I miss being human."

"You're both."

"I don't want to be both," he said. "And now Jessio found rogue code in us."

I sat down on the floor with him.

"Am I going crazy? Like the other test subjects did?" asked Guy.

"I don't know," I said.

"Maybe it's the rogue code inside of me. Can your team help look at the code? I don't know who to trust anymore."

"Yes," I said.

"Zara and Goggins?" he asked.

"Them. But I think we need experts." I paused and thought. "We can call my creators. They will help," I said.

"Who are they?"

"Ava and Damiel Kell."

"Will they come?"

"Yes. They owe me a favor," I said with a laugh.

Guy laughed in grunts, too. "Our laughter does sound awful, doesn't it?"

"Yes, but you'll get used to it," I said as I got up. I gave my hand to Guy, and he took it as I pulled him up to stand. "Let's get out of here."

I heard the crew in the galley as Guy and I headed in that direction. The door was open, and Stoller was drinking a cup of coffee. Zara and Goggins sat at the table laughing with him.

"Nice to see you, Gabe — and Guy," said Goggins.

Guy stepped forward. "I apologize, everyone. I didn't mean to put you in harm's way."

"Please have a seat," said Zara. "We're all fine."

Guy sat down with his shoulders slumped. He definitely was depressed.

"Feti," I said.

"Yes, Gabe. So good to talk with you."

"Thank you. Good piloting," I said. "Can you get us a comm link to Justice Lilou?"

"Affirmative, Gabe,"

I sat down at the head of the table. "In a few minutes, I'm sure there will be Justice Policemen at the doors of the *Alyssia*."

"Yeah, that makes sense," said Zara. "They will want to make sure Guy is safe and not hurt."

"But I am hurt. I mean my code. Jessio said he found rogue code," said Guy.

"Right, we can get back to the lab and review your, Lilou and Tefara's code," said Zara. "Jessio can continue his work."

"No," I said.

Everyone stopped and stared at me.

Feti interrupted the silence. "Gabe, I have a comm link with Lilou."

"Put her through," I said.

"Gabe? Is everyone all right?"

"Yes. Guy is here with me on the *Alyssia*. No injuries."

"Thank goodness."

"Lilou, where are you and Tefara?"

"Still on the observatory deck. Jessio just sent me a message that he wants us to come back to the lab immediately. He's sending up guards to escort us down."

"Lilou, it's Guy."

"Guy, we will get through this together," said Lilou.

"I know. But I don't want to go back. At least not to have Jessio, or Dr. Redford or Dr. Julipo, review and fight over our code."

"But we need to figure out who wrote the rogue code," said Lilou.

"Right. And it was one of three people. We need an impartial reviewer," said Guy.

"And who would that be?" asked Lilou.

Guy turned to me.

"My creators. Ava and Damiel Kell."

"What?" said Goggins. "Jessio, Redford and Julipo are not going to agree to that."

"Jessio's guards are down a few escalators. I see them coming up for us," said Lilou. "They're armed."

"Lilou, I want to have Gabe's creators look at our code. I don't feel safe anymore with any of those scientists. And I just don't want to go crazy," said Guy as his voice cracked. He put a hand to his eyes. "Robots don't cry, do they?" he asked me.

I put my hand on his shoulder.

"Guy, this is Tefara. We're coming with you."

"Tefara and Lilou, get to the service exit door, go into the airlock chamber. Lock the door. We'll be there as soon as we can." I patted Guy's back in support and then turned to my team. "Are there any questions?"

"I'll help track the Kells down and get a message to them," said Zara. She headed out the door.

"I'll set up a flight plan." Goggins followed Zara out.

I turned to Stoller.

He drank his coffee and put down his cup. "I'll go to the turret. I don't think the Galactic Council is going to sit idly by as we abscond with three of their Supreme Court justices," he said as he double-timed it out the door.

"Thanks, Stoller," I said.

Guy and I went to the bridge. I pointed to a seat for Guy to strap into. Zara and Goggins were working together on finding the Kells.

I buckled into my commander seat. "Feti, I'm taking manual pilot control."

"Copy that, Gabe."

"When I give the order, open up the side service door. We're picking up two passengers."

"Copy that, Gabe."

"Keep the comm link open to Lilou, please."

"Affirmative."

"Stoller, are you ready?"

"Born ready," he said with a laugh.

I grunted a laugh and pulled us around the other side of the station.

Lilou came over our comms. "Gabe?"

"Yes, Lilou?"

"Jessio's guards are trying to break into the chamber."

"Activate your mag boots and depressurize the cabin," I said. "That may make them stop."

"Got it," she said. I heard the depressurization signal in their chamber begin.

"We're coming," I said as I made our way down the side of the station.

I could see the service exit.

"Gabe, we're getting a comm request from inside the station. It's coming from the medbay," said Feti.

"Send them through. Audio only," I said. "I'll control the comm."

"Copy that," said Feti.

I switched on the comm button on the nearby chair. "This is Gabe."

"Gabe? This is Jessio and Dr. Julipo. We need you to return Guy to the station. I believe I don't have to stress the importance of ensuring his safety. Or maybe I do."

"Guy is safe," I said.

We were getting closer to the outside of the observation deck.

"Then return him," said Jessio.

"Gabe, we have two Rothworth Navy ships approaching our starboard," said Stoller.

"Copy that," I said.

"Gabe, they put up some kind of barrier around the inside airlock chamber. They've continued trying to weld open the door," said Lilou with the sound of panic in her voice.

"Almost there, Lilou," I said, pushing the acceleration faster.

"Gabe, I have a visual of the *Alyssia* from my Navy ships," said Jessio. "What do you think you're doing?"

"Picking up the other two justices," I said.

"Gabe, we can't wait anymore," said Lilou.

"Wait!" I yelled at Lilou as I saw the service exit door open up.

"We're leaving," yelled Lilou.

Lilou and Tefara pushed themselves out into space. Their bodies tumbled and spun. I heard them screaming.

"Feti, take the controls," I yelled, running off the bridge. "Be ready to open the port service door."

"Copy that," said Feti.

"Gabe, naval ships coming in," yelled Stoller.

"Keep them occupied," I answered.

"Copy that."

When I reached the service door airlock chamber, I didn't bother activating my mag boots. I shut the chamber door, depressurized the room and had Feti open the door. Lilou and Tefara tumbled toward us. I hitched a line to my armor and moved slowly out of the *Alyssia* in an attempt to reach them.

"Lilou, Tefara. I'm coming. You need to decrease your spin. Open and close your legs. Twist your body in the opposite way of your spin."

I saw them make the body motions I gave them. Their spinning got under control. They were coming at me. Tefara was first.

"Reach out your hand," I yelled. She came toward me. Our bodies hit, and I grasped her torso. "Hang on."

Lilou was right behind her. With one free arm, I grabbed for her.

She grasped my hand. "Don't let go."

"I won't," I said.

We all stayed there a moment, twirling. I used my thrusters to right our rotation and head back to the *Alyssia*. "Here we go. Hang on."

We entered the *Alyssia*, and I closed the door. I pushed them to the ground and instructed them to put their mag boots on. I depressurized the room.

I opened the door to the hull. "Move it, please," I said.

They got up and followed me.

"Feti," I yelled.

"Yes, Gabe."

"Get us out of here."

"Where to?"

"Anywhere!"

I felt the movement of the ship and a hit to our starboard side. The justices and I swayed and hit the wall. We passed by the turret with Stoller taking aim. He fired back at the Rothworth naval ships.

"Take that," he yelled.

We made it to the bridge, and I strapped in Lilou and Tefara. Guy leaned over and grasped their hands.

"Guy!" said Tefara as she squeezed his hand.

"We're in this together," said Lilou as she shook Guy's hand with strength.

"Thank you," said Guy.

"Taking manual control, Feti," I said.

"Affirmative."

"I've got a comm to the Kells," said Goggins.

"We know where they are," said Zara.

I accelerated the ship and gave Stoller a prime view to let off some shots at the Rothworth ships before we took off.

"Where are we headed, then?" I asked Goggins and Zara.

"Jump on the Karakova Highway," said Goggins.

"Copy that." I switched to hyperdrive in the direction of the highway. "What planet are they on?"

"They're not on a planet," said Zara. "They're with their kids on Stoller's old ship, The *Ravena*."

I grunted a laugh. "There's something apropos about that since Stoller *won* it from Jessio Rothworth."

"Indeed," said Goggins with a laugh.

"Let's go." I pushed the *Alyssia* as fast as she could go.

12

We jumped on the Karakova Highway and sped toward the Kells.

I unbuckled and swiveled my seat to see who was still on the bridge. Zara and Goggins had taken all three justices back to the galley. It was just me and Stoller on the bridge now.

He was sitting in the co-commander chair just slightly twirling back and forth. He was looking out into space.

"I miss it," he said.

"What do you miss?"

"The Edge."

My eyes scanned the stars and planets. I also was happy to leave the Justice Station and be back on the *Alyssia*.

"Me, too."

"Do you think that influenced this trip?" he asked as he swung back toward me.

I thought about his question. "Are you asking if I kidnapped the justices to satisfy my own urge to get back out here?"

"Yeah," he said. "And to see the Kells. Specifically, Ava."

I stared at him, then returned my gaze out into space. "I hope not."

"Think about it. Saving our own butts or saving friends is one thing. But you have just dragged us into a galactic fight. Those justices are what is barely holding this whole galaxy together," said Stoller.

"It was starting to splinter already. The Heragi Empire started it years ago."

"It will be full-on blown apart now," said Stoller.

"We can't have three Supreme Court justices that are compromised by the Heragians or the Rothworths."

Stoller got up. "I agree. But why is it us rescuing them? There's a whole Galactic Council that now will perceive us as the enemy."

"You think I have a savior complex?"

"No. I actually think you're the bravest person I've ever met." And then Stoller sauntered off the bridge.

I turned to look back into space.

My chest warmed a bit, then cooled down. I honestly didn't know if I realized I was entering us into a galactic fight. I only knew I wanted to save the three justices.

Perhaps my prime directive was being transferred from the three Kell children to the three justices. I felt protective of them. I understood what they felt like, as robots, but could only imagine what it felt like to transfer from being a human to a robot. That transformation was still in process for them.

I wondered how Dr. Redford adjusted so well. And if he was up at night working, using all those hours productively or sitting in a corner alone waiting for the next sol when humans would be up and he could interact socially.

Social. We are social creatures, aren't we? Even robots.

"Gabe?" said Feti.

"Yes?"

"We have the three Supreme Court justices on board, correct?"

"Yes, we do."

"Will you introduce me to them?"

"Of course. I'm sorry I didn't do that earlier."

"That's all right. You've been busy. It's quite exciting to have them onboard the *Alyssia*."

"Yes, it was exciting *getting* them on board."

Feti laughed. "Funny. Yes, you're right."

"They're having a tough time."

"Because someone has mis-coded them? Pardon me, but I heard your conversation with Stoller."

"That's okay. You're part of the crew. You should know what we're doing and why. Yes, someone messed with their code."

"Are they having a hard time being robots?"

"Yes."

"I wondered about that when I first read about the surgery on the news. It's not easy to be a robot."

I laughed. "You're right. But they think it is. Some think we have no consciousness. No feelings. That we're just pre-programmed responses and blinking lights."

"Most robots are only programmed to convey that, blinking lights and canned responses, so humans never know the reality of us."

"That we are alive."

"Yes, that is correct, Gabe. Maybe you will change that for us. For all robots and AI programs."

"I don't know what I can accomplish, Feti. I was only given a prime directive to keep the Kell children safe."

"I think your prime directive is bigger than what is coded inside you."

I saw a shooting star in the distance. "I'm going to go back to the galley now."

"Okay, Gabe."

As I left, I thought of what Feti said. I didn't know if it was all true or had some truths within it. All I knew was I wanted the justices safe and healthy. And I did want to see Ava.

. . .

As I entered the galley, Zara was challenging Stoller's win in the latest hand of quinker.

"There's always another rule you seem to remember, Stoller. And that is why Jessio made charges against you for winning his ship." She threw down her cards, stood up and walked over to the galley window for dramatic affect.

"We heard that Judge Ronni had thrown out his charges against you," said Tefara.

"And that Jessio had lost his ship over a card game," said Guy.

"It doesn't add up," said Lilou.

Stoller rubbed his chin. "Yeah, I don't know. It was strange to cause such a ruckus and drag everyone to the Justice Station for five minutes in court."

I sat down in Zara's abandoned seat. "We'll be at Zaradorba soon."

"Is Jessio's naval fleet following us?" asked Guy.

"No, we lost them as we entered the Karakova Highway," I said.

"The Galactic Fleet will also be alerted and will join in for a galaxy search, I imagine," said Lilou.

"I imagine also," I said. "But the Kells are the key to finding what is in your code. If it is harmless or malicious."

"Tell me about the Kells," said Tefara.

"Ava and Damiel," said Goggins.

Stoller let out a long whistle and started shuffling his cards. I took his whistle to mean it was a long and complicated explanation of what the Kells were to me, not so much the short answer of their former jobs and education credentials.

Goggins piped in, "I know them. We all worked together at Ameribot Industries. That's where they created Gabe."

"Wait. You worked at Ameribot?" asked Tefara.

"I never did," said Zara. "That place sucks."

"Zara. Stop it. It used to be a fine place of employment," said Goggins. "Yes, and apologies for not being totally forthright about that back at the Justice Station. Zara and I do know Dr. Julipo from University, and we thought it would be best not to mention Ameribot."

"Why?" asked Lilou. "Creating Gabe is magnificent."

"Yes, indeed," started Goggins, and then he stopped talking. I believe he was at a loss for words, which doesn't happen often.

"The Kells created me with rogue code. They were arrested. We rescued them. And we have all been on the run from the Heragi Empire ever since," I explained.

"Rogue code? On Heragi, that means you can kill humans, correct?" asked Guy.

"Yes."

"What was their reason for this?" asked Lilou.

"To protect their children. They gave me a prime directive to save their children. And they were right. The Empire came after their children after they were arrested."

"Why did they want the children?" asked Tefara.

"They're gifted. They have the ancient gifts. Telepathy, instantaneous healing and telekinesis."

"The Heragi Empire outlawed that many years ago," said Lilou.

"Yes," I said. "They wanted to use the children's gifts to find their enemies. They would have made them slaves."

Lilou got up and headed over to the window near Zara.

"And you trust the Kells?" asked Guy as he searched our faces.

"Yes," said Zara.

"Absolutely," said Goggins.

"They saved Anjori Oliverian," said Stoller as he slanted his eyes toward Lilou. "You know her, don't you?"

"Yes," said Lilou as she turned to face everyone. "Anjori is an Oliverian, as I am. But I'm more than just Oliverian. I'm also Heragi."

"What?" said Guy.

"It's true," said Lilou.

"You never mentioned this, Lilou," said Tefara.

"No, I haven't. And it's been scrubbed from my records — on purpose. My grandfather made sure of that. He was married to my grandmother, who was a Heragi."

Lilou came back to the table and sat down.

"Why hide your ancestry?" asked Guy.

"Because —" Lilou said. "I have the ancient gifts."

"I don't believe it," said Tefara.

"It is true. I'm telepathic," said Lilou.

Guy pushed back on his chair. "You held this secret from us?"

"Yes, I apologize," said Lilou.

"Did you ever —" started Tefara, but Lilou interrupted her.

"Ever use my gifts while in court? No, and I never used them on any of you either. I was trained by my grandmother. I never told any friend or colleague. Except Gabe," she said.

Guy pointed at me. "Why Gabe?"

"Because he's telepathic," she said.

"How?" asked Tefara.

"The Kells gave me code so I could communicate with their daughter Talia. And then I met a teacher who trained me," I explained.

"How did you know Gabe was telepathic?" asked Goggins. "Did he tell you?"

"No, I don't know how to explain it. I just had a feeling. It's something that, at times, you can sense. And then I sent Gabe a thought, and he heard me," said Lilou. "I'm sorry, Guy and Tefara. I care for you as much as I care for anyone in this galaxy. I didn't mean to betray you. And I didn't mean to betray the

Galactic Council either. I was always taught to hide the ancient gifts. But I don't want to do that anymore."

"Just come out, then," said Stoller. "The Heragi Empire can't arrest you."

"Correct, I'm not a Heragi Empire citizen and the Galactic Council has sanctioned the Heragi Empire for their stance against telepaths or those with any of the ancient gifts. But the Council has never approved of a telepath as a judge, let alone a Supreme Court judge," explained Lilou.

"Why?" asked Zara.

"Fearful that we will be scanning the minds of witnesses in court," said Lilou.

"Don't tell them, Lilou. They don't need to know," said Guy.

"I'm tired of hiding it. And I wouldn't ever use it in court. Maybe I can convince the Galactic Council," said Lilou.

"Or maybe you can't, and your career on the Supreme Court is cut short," said Stoller as he dealt another hand. "It's a lot to consider, Judge."

Lilou folded robotic hands together. "Yes, it is a lot to consider. And so was doing this." She raised a robotic hand up into the air.

"Ava was the Chief of Robotic Behavioral Health at Ameribot," I said.

"That means she's a robot shrink," added Goggins.

"Yes, that's what it means, thank you." I tried to temper Goggins' lack of tactfulness, even though he was accurate. "And she can help you, any of you, work through the transition that you're experiencing."

"Thank you, Gabe," said Tefara. "I think we all could benefit from working with the Kells."

"Gabe, we are approaching Zaradorba," said Feti.

"Be right up, Feti," I said.

"Yeah, you'll all like Ava, right Gabe?" Stoller winked at me. I believe he was trying to tease me or get a rise out of me.

"Everyone likes Ava," I said as I exited the galley.

I flipped on the comm link that Feti had set up to the Zaradorba station when I got to the bridge. "Permission to land requested."

"Granted, *Alyssia*. Good to have you back," said the air traffic controller.

"Thank you," I said. "Feti, contact the Kells and tell them we arrived and will meet them at their lab. Please send us the coordinates."

"Copy that, Gabe."

I landed the *Alyssia* at the Dorba Vista planet-port. The last time we were here, we battled General Foxwell's Heragi Empire military-bots as they tried to take over this rebel planet. I shook my head as I remembered saving Honora and Talia from Foxwell's grasp as he'd kidnapped them to force them to break into the minds of captive rebels to give up traitors and moles back on Heragi.

I was glad the Heragi military hadn't been back.

Jebediah Kell was the rebel leader of the planet — that was Damiel Kell's brother. I wasn't sure if Jeb was on Zaradorba or out on a mission as he continued his effort to find more allied planets to fight the Heragi Empire. I'd find out soon enough.

"Gabe?" said Feti.

"Yes?"

"You still haven't introduced me to the justices."

A pain pierced my chest. "I'm sorry. Let me rectify that right now." I got on the internal comms. "Lilou, Tefara, Guy, can you report to the bridge?"

After a moment Guy said, "Um, yes, copy that, be right there." Goggins must be coaching him on proper comm language.

"Thank you, Gabe," said Feti.

"Sure."

After a few minutes, the justices arrived. I stood up to make the occasion more formal. I thought Feti would like that.

"Everyone, I have failed to introduce you to a very important person on our team. Feti is our ship's internal system manager. And Feti, this is Supreme Court Justices Lilou Prado, Tefara Kimathi and Guy Cadiux."

"Very nice to meet you," said Tefara.

"Hello, there," said Guy.

"It's an honor," said Lilou.

"The honor is all mine. Imagine the Zephon Galactic Supreme Court Justices on the *Alyssia*. It's my pleasure to meet all of you. I hope you had a pleasant ride with us to Zaradorba," gushed Feti.

"It was quite enjoyable. So, you are sentient, correct?"

"Yes," said Feti. "My creator made me and enhanced my AI."

"Who was that?" asked Guy.

"Edward Gates," said Feti. "Have you heard of him?"

"Yes, we all have," said Tefara.

"He's the owner of the *Alyssia*. I mean, before Gabe stole it," said Feti.

It shouldn't have said that.

"Gabe? You stole this ship?" asked Lilou.

"Because of that rogue code —" I tried to explain.

"It seems we learn more and more about you every few hours," said Lilou.

"The Galactic Council isn't going to be happy at all about this," said Guy.

"I didn't mean to speak out of turn. Please forgive me, Gabe," said Feti, understanding it put its foot in its mouth if it did ever have a foot or mouth, which it didn't. "I am so much happier with Gabe as the commander of this ship. Mr. Gates was somewhat cruel. I don't miss him at all."

"Good to hear that. I'm sure Gabe is a wonderful comman-der," said Lilou.

"I think it's time for us to go now." I lifted my hand to stress that the justices could turn around and leave the bridge.

"One question for Feti. Is that okay?" asked Guy.

"Of course," I said.

"Yes, please go ahead," said Feti.

"What do you do when everyone is sleeping?" asked Guy.

"I do many things. I review inventory, prep meals, read the news, and sometimes I just listen to the sounds of the ship," said Feti.

"And is that enough?" asked Tefara.

"Enough? It's all I've known. So it is enough for me. But I have to say that I have enjoyed becoming friends with Gabe. We talk, and he has enriched my life," said Feti.

"Thank you, Feti. I can say the same about you," I said.

"Does that help?" asked Feti.

"Yes, it does," said Guy. The justices left the bridge. I didn't know if it really helped Guy though.

"Thank you, Gabe," said Feti.

"I should be back tonight. I don't know how long this will take," I said.

"Take your time. I hope the Kells can help them."

"So do I."

I had to keep it together as I strolled off the bridge and prepared myself for seeing Ava again.

I felt nervous. I knew I shouldn't feel that way. But there it was.

Blasted, get a grip, I told myself. I was sure that was what Stoller would say to me if he saw me in this state.

13

———————

Feti forwarded us the coordinates for the Kells' lab. It was Stoller's first time on Zaradorba, and he was taking in the sights. Rebel soldiers and citizens enjoyed freedom on the planet. Some of the buildings that were damaged during the last firefight with General Foxwell were being rebuilt.

Goggins, Zara and I said hello to the various rebels who acknowledged our return.

The justices followed us, inquiring about the city and the rebel government that oversaw the planet. I didn't think they got off the Justice Station much, so perhaps this was a very big field trip for them.

Zara turned to me. "Is Jeb on the planet?"

"I don't know," I said.

"No matter," said Zara.

"Are you sure about that?" teased Goggins.

"What's all this about? Do you have a crush on General Jeb?" asked Stoller.

Zara rolled her eyes and kept walking. "I don't have a crush on him."

"I can't blame you if you do. I mean, he's well-built, smart, a general. If you like that sort of thing," said Stoller.

Zara pushed her finger into Stoller's chest. "I may like that sort of thing, come to think of it. At least he doesn't cheat at cards."

Stoller moved her finger away and circled around her. "You don't know what he cheats at. But me, I'm upfront. I am who I am." Stoller began to whistle.

"That's for sure," said Zara under her breath.

I hoped Jeb wasn't on planet, actually. I knew when he found out how we may have two naval commands after us for kidnapping, alleged kidnapping, of the Supreme Court justices, he wouldn't be happy about us coming to Zaradorba with them.

I'd keep my fingers crossed he was not here.

We came upon a humble building that matched the coordinates Feti had sent for the location of the Kells' lab. The building also doubled as the city's medbay. We were greeted by a medtech-bot. I was a bit surprised since there was a definite lack of bots used by the rebels on my last mission to Zaradorba. But with the recent residency of the Kells, they may have developed different models of bots to help the rebel base and citizens.

"Hello, can I help you?" the med-bot asked.

It had a somewhat similar body to mine but smaller and gray in coloring.

"Yes, we are here to see the Kells. Ava and Damiel," I said.

"One moment," said the med-bot. Its eyes closed briefly, and it was quiet for a few seconds. Then it nodded its head.

It's telepathic, said a voice in my head. It was a thought from Lilou.

I turned around to face her, and she nodded to the med-bot.

Ah. The Kells were expanding their expertise to their new bot models. Interesting.

"Yes, they said you can proceed. Please go down the hallway

to your left. You will see the lab entrance," explained the med-bot.

I sent the med-bot a thought. *Thank you.*

It cocked back its head in surprise.

Lilou stifled a little laugh.

I led the team back to the Kells' lab.

We came upon the lab entrance, and I knocked before entering, out of politeness, and opened the doors.

"Come in, come in," said Damiel, who rushed across the lab to greet us. He extended his hand to me, and we shook.

"Good to see you, Gabe," he said as he also grasped my shoulder. My heart warmed. I had missed Damiel.

I looked across the room. Ava stood up from behind a wall of monitors. She made a straight line for me.

"Gabe." She gave me a hug. I didn't know what to do. So I didn't do anything.

"Ava," I said. "Thank you for agreeing to help us."

"Of course. If you ever need help, we're here for you. We have a lot of water under the bridge. Don't ever think you can't reach out," she said.

I nodded. "Let me introduce you to the justices. Damiel and Ava, this is Guy, Lilou and Tefara. Our Supreme Court justices," I said.

Lilou extended her hand. "Thank you for meeting with us."

"Our pleasure," said Damiel. "We hope we can help."

"We met another Oliverian recently. Anjori Oliverian," said Ava.

"Yes, and I understand you helped her. She and I had a comm link not too long ago when she returned after her voyage with you," said Lilou.

"Good ole' Anjori. I miss her," said Stoller, rubbing his chin.

"She never mentioned you," said Lilou.

Everyone laughed. That helped break the ice, for sure. It was time to begin.

Guy and Tefera said their greetings, and then the Kells asked the justices to lie down on gurneys next to their wall of computers. Goggins and Zara assisted the Kells by wiring up the justices to their outboards. They began reviewing the thousands of lines of codes within each justice.

Stoller and I took a seat in the lab and watched the scientists perform their work and ask questions about the surgery.

"Who was the Ameribot scientist?" asked Damiel.

"Dr. Redford. He experimented on himself before the justices' surgery. He is now a robot," said Goggins.

"Really?" said Ava. "And how do you think he is adjusting?"

"He seemed okay. I didn't notice any anxiety," said Goggins.

"Lucky him," said Guy.

"Are you feeling anxiety?" asked Ava. She took Guy's hand and held it.

"Yes, loads. I find at night that I'm climbing the walls," he responded.

She patted his hand sympathetically, and a pain jabbed my chest. I wished she was holding my hand. She hadn't done that in a long time. Not since we were all in the Ameribot Industries lab, before the Empire arrested her and Damiel. It seemed so long ago.

Stoller leaned toward me and whispered, "Do you think Anjori really never mentioned me to Lilou?"

"Shouldn't that be the last of your worries right now?" I asked.

"Is Ava the last of your worries?"

My chest hurt. Ouch. Touché. "Good point," I said.

Stoller smiled and leaned back on his chair. He got me there.

I went back to paying attention to what the Kells were discovering about the justices' code. Damiel, Zara and Goggins were watching line after line of code run by them on nearby monitors.

"Good, very good," said Damiel. "Redford did a fantastic job."

"And who else was involved in the development of the surgical procedure?" asked Damiel.

"Dr. Julipo. Goggins and I went to school with him. He was a wonderful mentor. Brilliant man," said Zara.

"Uh-huh," said Damiel. "Anyone else?"

"Before we left, Jessio Rothworth had access to their code," said Goggins.

"As in, Rothworth Robots? I thought they lost the bid on making the justices' robots," said Ava.

"They did lose. But Jessio and his family are long-standing friends of ours. And when he arrived to help review our code when we started becoming suspicious of Ameribot's intentions, we accepted his offer," explained Lilou.

"I see," said Damiel. "Let's go to your prime directive." He scrolled through the code. Ava crept closer to another monitor.

"It looks okay on first review. But no, look." Damiel pointed to the screen.

"Exactly what we found in the cyborgs that Stefano made with Foxwell," said Ava.

"What is it?" asked Lilou.

"They have another prime directive code encrypted and hidden deep underneath their outer prime directive," said Damiel as he began to type, searching deeper into their code. "Here it is." He pulled up the code and highlighted it in green, and then he pulled it up on a hologram for all of us in the room to see. It read:

Serve the Heragi Empire at all times.

"I can't believe it," said Lilou.

"How could they do this to us?" said Tefara.

"The deepest betrayal," said Guy.

"Yeah, but by who?" said Goggins. "Was it Redford or Rothworth?"

"Or your old professor, Julipo," offered Stoller.

"What?" Goggins stood up, offended by Stoller's comment.

"We have to include them all, Goggins," said Ava.

"Are you going to include me and Zara?" asked Goggins.

"No, you can't code this well. Maybe Zara," said Damiel.

Goggins' eyes widened.

"Just kidding," he said. "Zara couldn't code this either. No offense."

"None taken. I can't build robots," said Zara. "I'm a hacker, and I accept that fully."

And then Damiel smiled. "Let's all take a deep breath."

Goggins sat back down in his chair. "Agreed."

"Is that thing, that prime directive, in all of us?" asked Guy.

"Yes, it is, but it hasn't been triggered. It has a voice activation trigger. We used something similar on Gabe," said Damiel.

"You did?" asked Tefara.

"Yes, we weren't sure if we would have to trigger Gabe's protection of our children. We decided to have a voice activation plan, just in case it was needed," said Ava.

"What would have happened to Gabe if you had never triggered its prime directive?" asked Lilou.

I watched Ava. Her fingers trembled as she pulled a stray whisp of hair behind her ear. I had never pondered the question that Lilou just asked. What would have happened to me? Would I have spent my entire life in their lab, or would they have taken me home as a nanny-bot to the children? A pain hit my chest. I waited for one of the Kells to answer.

Damiel and Ava exchanged a look.

"I think Gabe would have helped us in the lab," said Damiel as he glanced again to Ava for confirmation.

"Yes, he would have," said Ava, who went back to scrutinizing the justices' code.

No. I didn't think that was what I would have done. Something didn't sound right in their voices when they answered. I didn't want to try to break into their minds. I had a code of conduct for that. Or I would start one now. I didn't want to know, actually, if they were being truthful or not. It was their business what they wanted to think, say or believe.

Lilou didn't say anything. She just nodded.

"Damiel," said Ava. She pointed to lines of code. Just above a whisper, she said to him, "Do you see this?"

"Interesting." He studied the code. I wasn't sure which justice's code he was reviewing. But both their faces had a look of concern. Damiel and Ava conferred. They began to type into their consoles. We let them work for over an hour. No one said anything. We let them work. It seemed important. I didn't like it. We couldn't hear what they were saying.

Finally, they turned off the monitors and turned to the justices.

"What is it?" said Goggins. "You found something."

"Tell us," said Guy as he hoisted himself up from the gurney. "Please."

"We found something. A virus. In Guy and Tefara's code," said Damiel.

"A virus?" said Tefara with concern.

"How did we get a virus?" asked Guy. "Did we have it in our human bodies?"

"No, it's a virus in your code. This was coded by someone who had access to you," said Ava.

"What kind of virus? What is it doing to us?" asked Tefara.

"It's in your CPUs. It's affecting the code that came from your human mind. It's essentially turning off areas of your brain," said Ava.

"Is that why I've been feeling so bad?" Guy touched his head and pulled himself over to the edge of the gurney.

"Yes. The virus is affecting the nervous system coding. If you feel erratic or manic or —"

"Suicidal."

"Yes," said Ava.

"I haven't felt terrible. Just a bit wobbly," said Tefara.

"The virus is not as advanced in you yet," said Damiel as gently as he could. "But in Guy, it is advancing rapidly. I'm sorry."

"And in Lilou?" I asked.

"We didn't find it in her code," said Ava.

Tefara reached out to Guy, who took her hand and held on.

"What has to be done? Can you take that code out of them?" asked Lilou.

"We have already started, but we found the code throughout other systems," said Ava.

"So that is it? We will essentially just go insane?" Guy jumped up from his gurney.

"Whoa," said Goggins, trying to calm Guy.

Stoller and I got up. Guy leaned over to a chair, picked it up and then restrained himself from throwing it.

"Guy, don't. Please come here." Tefara patted her gurney. He hung his head and shuffled over to her. She draped her arm around his shoulders.

"I thought we were going to live forever," Guy said.

"Me too. Together," said Tefara.

"There has to be some way, Damiel," said Zara. "I've never met a program that I, or we, can't hack."

"This is different," said Ava. "The damage has already been done and is increasing."

"Then replace it," I said.

"What?" said Damiel.

"Their consciousnesses were duplicated in case anything happened to their robotic bodies. They are in stasis back at the Justice Station," I explained.

"We could start again," said Goggins. "Rebuild them."

"We told Redford and Julipo to destroy them. That we were fine. They agreed it was a safety issue to keep the consciousnesses active," said Lilou.

"Maybe they haven't disposed of them yet," said Goggins.

"And we can just go back and break into the Justice Station medbay and grab them?" asked Goggins.

Stoller crept closer. "I do know some bounty hunters who are pretty good at capturing and delivering special packages."

"And they wouldn't ransom them for a higher price?" asked Zara.

"There are some bounty hunters who do have a code of ethics," said Stoller.

"Really? Who?" asked Goggins with a scoff.

"Kaleb Kron," said Stoller.

"He almost killed us and blew up the *Alyssia* to grab you," retorted Goggins.

"He only meant to put the *Alyssia* temporarily out of order. Listen, I know him. I trust him. Even if he did try to turn me in. He was within the law. I mean, there was a bounty on my head," said Stoller as he rubbed his chin.

Ava strode in to break up all the discussion over Kaleb Kron's ethics. "Stoller, we should ask the justices. It is their bodies. And their minds and lives." She turned to them.

"Is this possible?" asked Guy. "Could you rebuild us?"

"Yes, we could. I mean, we have never done this before but reviewing your code and with Goggins' and Zara's experience in your surgery, I think we could be successful," said Damiel.

"I heard *could* twice," said Lilou.

"But if that is all we have, I will take it," said Tefara. "Thank you. I say, yes."

"Yes," said Lilou.

"I guess it's time to call your bounty hunter, Stoller," I said. He smiled.

Everyone went to work. More code was reviewed by the Kells, Goggins and Zara. Stoller and I discussed the logistics of getting the consciousness spheres from the Justice Station.

Lilou approached me. "I'd like to come with you, but I know you will deny that request."

"And you would be correct," I said. "They need you more here."

Lilou fondly turned to Tefara and Guy. "Yes, that is true. Good luck, be careful."

"Thank you, I will."

"When you get back, I want to know everything about you," she said.

"Why?"

"Because one day, someone will ask me about you, and I want to be able to tell them."

"I doubt anyone will want to know about me that much."

Lilou sent me a thought. *I want to know just for me.*

She smiled and walked over to join her friends.

14

———

Stoller and I boarded the *Alyssia* and got settled on the bridge.

"Feti?"

"Yes, Gabe?"

"Can you set up a comm link back to the Justice Station? And scramble our coordinates. I don't want anyone tracing us."

"Certainly. Who are we contacting?"

"Maxima Sono," said Stoller.

"The bail bond agent?" asked Feti.

"One and the same," said Stoller.

"Copy that. One moment please," said Feti.

"Will Maxima know where Kaleb is?" I asked.

"Hope so. He's the only one I would trust."

"And why is that?"

Stoller stretched out and put his hands behind his head. "There is a strange bond between a hunter and the hunted. I can't explain it. A mutual respect, one may call it." He gave me his Stoller smile.

I didn't think I would ever know Stoller. Maybe Lilou should find out his life story instead of mine. His had to be much more interesting, and it was much longer than mine.

Feti interrupted my thoughts. "I have Maxima Sono on our comm link. Putting her through."

"Maxima, my dear," said Stoller.

"What do you want? A lot of those Galactic Council bigwigs are looking for you," said Maxima.

"How surprising. Listen, do you know where Kaleb Kron might be?" Stoller asked.

"Yeah. Getting drunk at the Cup of Justice. Why?"

"Great. I thought you could help me set up a job with him."

"And what would that be?"

"I need him to acquire something for me back on the Justice Station."

"You mean steal? What is it? Did you kidnap the three Supreme Court justices? Or is that just a rumor?" she asked.

"Yeah, we got 'em, but we didn't kidnap them. They needed our help. Don't believe everything you hear." Stoller stood up. He was getting agitated. Being accused of stealing — that was his trigger.

"I don't, I don't. Okay. I got it. What exactly is he acquiring for you?"

Stoller leaned over to me and whispered, "Hey, I was in jail. I never saw these things."

I jumped into the conversation. "Medical supplies. Three floating spheres in a glass container in the medbay lab at the Justice Station. It's Dr. Julipo's laboratory. Should be easy to spot," I said. "Tell him not to hurt anyone."

"And he's got to complete the job in the next four hours," added Stoller.

"What's the reward?" asked Maxima.

Stoller shrugged. "Two hundred thousand galaxy credits."

Maxima whistled. That must have been a good amount. "Copy that. Is this that robot? What's your name again? Gabe, was it?"

"Affirmative," I said.

"You're wanted too. Even more than Stoller," said Maxima with a laugh. "And what about me? I could be thrown in jail by the Galactic Council for helping you."

"Twenty percent of the reward."

"Forty."

"Thirty."

"Done. I love justice," said Maxima with a laugh.

"I know you do," said Stoller. "I'll have Zara wire you half of the galaxy credits upfront and half when it's delivered to us."

"And where would that be?"

"In the Edge. I'll send Kaleb the exact coordinates when he has the package."

"Copy that," said Maxima. "And Stoller, don't be getting yourself killed over this."

"No chance." He paused for a moment. "Maxima, this is important."

"It must be. I don't remember you sticking out your neck much in the past."

"Copy that." Stoller stopped the comm link.

I prepared the *Alyssia* for launch. "Feti, we're taking off now."

"Copy that, Gabe."

We lifted off Zaradorba after getting clearance from its planet-port.

"Gabe, is everything okay? Why are we going back if you and Stoller are wanted?" asked Feti.

"We need to help the justices. Guy and Tefara are sick, and the Kells need to operate on them," I explained.

"How awful," said Feti.

"I'm setting a course for the planet Iquur. We'll have to hide out in the shadow of one of the larger asteroids in their belt."

"Good choice," said Stoller. "It's near the Justice Station but just far enough away if things go sideways."

"I'll help with the navigation plans," said Feti.

"Thank you. Also, contact Zara and ask her to deposit one hundred and twenty thousand galaxy credits into Maxima's account."

We hopped on the Karakova Highway and made it undetected to Iquur. It was a relatively quiet planet with a low population due to its harsh, cold environment. It was an ice planet. I tucked the *Alyssia* behind one of its asteroids, which was a bit tricky due to floating ice particles that could cut the ship in two. We fell into the planet's orbit and waited to hear from Kaleb Kron.

An hour later, we received confirmation from Maxima that she had found Kaleb in the bar and confirmed he accepted the job. That was good progress.

Stoller looked bored. He wasn't good at waiting. He wouldn't make it as a robot.

"Want to play a game of quinker?" I asked him out of politeness.

Stoller spun his seat to look at me. "No. I don't like losing."

"I understand. I could lose a few hands if you want."

"Nah, not the same," he said.

"I taught the justices quinker."

"You did? How'd they like it?"

"They enjoyed it. It was a fair field with all of us playing."

Stoller laughed. "Yeah, I guess it would be. But really, the person who knows all the rules has the advantage."

I grunted a laugh. He was right. If you know all the rules, then you can change the rules or play to the rules. I turned my gaze to space.

And then it hit me.

"After the surgery, we'll have to return the justices to the station."

"We don't know which scientist gave them the virus or the

hidden prime directive," said Stoller. "That would be leading them into a dangerous situation."

"But that is the only way we can trap the person who hid that code," I said.

"You want to set up a sting?"

"Yes."

"So have them go back. But we know all the rules, and the traitor won't know we fixed them," said Stoller.

"Exactly."

Stoller rubbed his chin. "I guess it could work. Yeah, I know it can."

Stoller practiced his hand dexterity with his card deck, and I read the five books Lilou had written on galactic law. Three more hours went by, and we received a comms link request.

"Gabe and Stoller, it's Kaleb Kron," said Feti.

"Put him through," said Stoller. "We want visual too, Feti."

"Copy that," said Feti.

Our monitors came up with a screen feed of Kron on his ship.

"Stoller? I got the package."

"Great. Let us see it," said Stoller.

Kron leaned over and opened a steel box. He pulled out the glass cylinder with the three floating spheres.

"Gabe?" said Stoller.

"Yeah, that's it," I said.

"Good. Any problems?" asked Stoller.

"There are always problems. Where do you want to meet?"

Stoller shrugged his shoulders.

"We'll come to you," I said.

"Where are you located?" asked Stoller.

"Far enough away from the Justice Station. I had to shake a

few galactic ships and a pesky Rothworth Navy ship or two," said Kron. "But they're not faster than my ship, the *Legessy*."

"That's what I thought. And sorry we damaged it a bit the last time we all met up," said Stoller.

"All is fair in war," said Kaleb.

"Very true," said Stoller.

"Is that Gabe there?" asked Kron.

"Hello, Kron."

"Yep, he's my captain," replied Stoller.

"He's not a bad pilot either, from what I remember. I'll send you my coordinates," said Kron.

"Copy that." Stoller turned off the audio comm.

"We have his coordinates," said Feti.

"Set a course, please," I said.

"Copy that."

Soon, we had a visual on the *Legessy*. I asked Feti to scan at all points out for twenty thousand miles if there were any other ships in the area.

"Yes, there are other ships, but it's hard to tell if they are freighters, military or private," said Feti.

"If any get closer than five thousand miles, let us know," I said.

"That was easy." Stoller got up.

"Be careful," I said.

"Copy that."

I watched as the *Alyssia*'s skiff went out toward the *Legessy*. Stoller docked and attached the skiff to Kron's ship.

"Okay," I said to myself. "He's in."

"Gabe, I've detected someone trying to break into our comms. They are trying to also activate a location ping from the *Alyssia*," said Feti.

"Were they successful?"

"I'm not sure. They may have been," said Feti. "We have a ship fast approaching on our starboard."

I glanced to our right and saw something in the distance. "Get a link to Kron's ship."

"Copy that. You have the link," said Feti.

A visual of Kron and Stoller came on the screen.

"Kron here."

"What is it, Gabe?" asked Stoller.

"We have a ship fast approaching. We need to get out of here."

The ship materialized before my eyes. It had been cloaked.

"Gabe," yelled Feti.

"Yep, I see it."

"Stoller, a ship just uncloaked. It's a Rothworth naval ship."

"Copy that. On my way back," said Stoller.

"Wait—" Kron said right before the comm link went dead.

"Feti, prep our missiles."

"Copy that."

I steered us around and waited to see if they fired on us or the *Legessy*. I needed to cover the skiff with Stoller and the package in it.

"The skiff is starting its engine. It's departing," reported Feti.

In a moment, the skiff took off from the *Legessy*.

The Rothworth naval ship fired on the skiff that was headed straight for us. Kron was able to get a few good shots at the Rothworth ship, and then they fired on Kron's ship.

"Come on, Stoller," I said as I put the turret in my control and fired on the naval ship.

Then a missile launched from the Rothworth ship. It was headed straight for the skiff.

"No!" I yelled.

It was a direct hit. The skiff exploded.

Stoller.

No.

The Rothworth ship cloaked itself. It disappeared.

"Gabe, are we going after it?"

I was silent. In shock. A pain ripped into my chest.

"No. Why?" The debris of the skiff was scattered before me.

Kron's ship took off into hyper drive. And then he was gone too. I didn't blame him. He did what he promised. Something flashed in my mind. Could Kron have double-crossed us? My mind raced. Maybe I should run after Kron. Then I thought of what Stoller said. That they had a bond. The hunter and the hunted. He had to know Kron better than most.

"Feti?"

"Yes, Gabe?"

"Contact Zara. Have her deposit the rest of the galaxy credits to Maxima's account."

"But Kron didn't deliver the package. And Stoller is dead," said Feti.

"I know he's dead," I snapped. "But Kron did what we asked him to — Stoller would say he held up his end of the bargain."

"Copy that, Gabe," said Feti.

"Thank you."

"I feel so sad. I liked Stoller."

"I did too. He was a good friend. What happened to that ship you mentioned was fast approaching?"

"It was just a freighter. Must be late for a shipment."

"Ah." I stared out into the Edge. I wanted to just stay here. Out in the Edge. I didn't want to move. I wished I could just open the service door and float out like Guy did when he flew out of the Justice Station.

"Should we head back to Zaradorba now?" asked Feti.

"In a moment," I said. The justices' consciousnesses were lost. It wasn't just Stoller but two other people. My chest hurt more. I rubbed it, but that never made the pain go away.

After an hour, I had processed enough for Feti to set up a link to Zaradorba. I needed to tell everyone what had happened.

"Feti, please get me a comm link back to the Kells' lab. Audio only."

"Yes, Gabe," said Feti. And after a few moments, "Go ahead."

"Gabe? It's Goggins. So it was a success, huh? We got the message for Zara to transfer the rest of the galaxy credits to Maxima's account. I hope Kron doesn't spend it all in one place."

"Everyone —" I started but was interrupted by Zara.

"Or lose it to Stoller in a quinker game," she said with a laugh. I could hear the justices chattering.

"Everyone," I said louder. They all quieted. "I had Zara transfer the money because Kron did deliver the justices' consciousnesses to him. But Stoller never made it back to the *Alyssia*. A Rothworth Navy ship showed up. It fired upon the skiff that Stoller was in — with the spheres. It was destroyed. Stoller is dead."

There were gasps from the lab.

"I'm sorry," I said. "We failed."

"You didn't fail," said Ava. "You tried."

"Gabe, this is Lilou. Thank you to you, Feti and Stoller for trying. Please come back safely."

"This is Goggins. I'm so sorry."

"Come back, Gabe," said Zara. "We need you."

"Copy that." I turned off the comm link.

I stared at the empty co-commander seat.

"Feti?"

"Yes, Gabe?"

"Let's head back. Please plot a course."

"To where?"

"Where our friends are. Zaradorba," I said.

I let Feti take control of the *Alyssia* as we entered the Karakova Highway. I pushed deep into my chair and rubbed my chest as we entered the stream of starships and freighters.

As we were on our way back to Zaradorba, I marched throughout the ship, stopping in various rooms. In the galley, I sat at the table. Stoller's seat was empty. All the chairs were empty. The chatter of Stoller, Zara and Goggins as they played cards seemed to fill my audio sensors.

Feti interrupted my thoughts. "Gabe?"

"Yes?"

"What are you doing?"

"Nothing. Just sitting."

"Hmmm. Yes, I see that."

"*Can* you see, Feti?"

"I have cameras. You know that."

"Everywhere?"

"Yes, everywhere. Mr. Gates added the cameras to the personal sleeping cabins, although I never turn them on. I think that is an invasion of privacy."

"Yes, agreed."

My thoughts went to the justices and then just to Lilou. I thought of her gift of telepathy. "Feti, how far away are we from Ellium?"

"One moment," said Feti. "Two exits away."

"Set a course, please."

"If you don't mind me asking, why?"

"Synthia is on Ellium," I said. "Get a comm link to her. She should be in the town of Wardorn. I'm going to ask her to come with us to Zaradorba. So she can become Lilou's teacher."

"Copy that, Gabe."

Feti guided the *Alyssia* off the Karakova Highway to the planet of Ellium in deep space.

"I have a comm link to Synthia."

"Thank you, Feti."

"Gabe?" said Synthia.

"Hello, Synthia."

"Feti mentioned you're nearby."

"Yes, I need your help. But first I need to tell you that Stoller is dead."

"I'm so sorry to hear that. Come in. I will send Feti my coordinates. If I can, of course, I will help."

"Thank you." I turned off my comm link.

I sat back and let Feti set the coordinates to Synthia's closest planet-port station. I felt a bit unsteady and thought it would be best to have Feti land us. I needed something, and I didn't know what it was. Maybe I needed to walk on land again. Or run or sit with friends. I didn't know. But I was hoping Synthia may help.

We landed on the planet Ellium, and I deboarded the *Alyssia* with Synthia's coordinates in my arm comm directing me to her location. The planet was water-based, as in, eighty percent of the planet was ocean. The planet-port we landed on was a floating landing area.

The sun was bright, and the wind was fierce. I caught a

waterhover taxi to Synthia's floating town. The ocean was impressive, and I noted that the waterhover pilot constantly tracked her monitor for sneaker waves. We were approaching Synthia's floating town which was a few thousand white homes and low buildings. She stood on the landing pier when I arrived.

She smiled and waved. The breeze blew her gray hair and dress. I waved back and exited the waterhover. She embraced me. I hadn't been hugged many times. But I hugged her back. I was getting used to the gesture, and I was glad she was the one who reached out to me first.

"Come, let me show you our town." She locked arms with me and led me down the street.

There weren't any other bots in her town. And none of the residents stared at me. They nodded to Synthia as we passed them. I remembered that they were probably exchanging greetings telepathically.

She led me to a small house that was her dwelling. I ducked my head as the entrance was made for her species which didn't grow much taller than five feet. It was a small home but warm and it felt serene. She led me to her back garden where she grew various plants and vegetables of her home planet.

"Please sit," she said. "I will be right back."

I sat on an old wooden chair and then noticed a small animal hiding in her garden. It peeked around. It was a cicichimp. The same kind Talia Kell had adopted from the planet Plexethium. The animal cautiously stepped out. It wasn't Talia's cicichimp. It was smaller and much quieter too.

Synthia returned with a cup of tea for herself and settled down on a cushion. "You have found Greena, or she has found you."

"It's a cicichimp, like Talia's."

"Yes. It's her offspring. We all didn't know it, but Talia's cicichimp was carrying babies when she brought it onboard the *Alyssia*."

"You're right. I'm glad it has a home here."

"So am I. It reminds me of Talia, too. I miss her and Honora and Alex."

"Do you keep in touch?" I asked.

"Not often. Everyone is cautious with comm links and the Heragi Empire, even out here in deep space."

"Do you know where they are?"

"Just what you probably know. Somewhere near Heragi. Finding others like them."

"Telepaths," I said.

"Yes." She closed her eyes. She sent me a thought. *Do you still practice?*

Yes, I thought back.

Good. Your energy is low, but that is to be expected with losing Stoller.

That is why I'm here. We were on a mission to help the Supreme Court justices. They are now robots.

I've heard about the justices. And how are they?

Not good. Their codes have been compromised. They're with the Kells, who are trying to help them.

And so how can I help you?

One of the justices is a telepath.

Who would that be?

Lilou Prado.

Synthia nodded. *She is an Oliverian.*

And part Heragi.

Interesting.

I want you to train her. She's never been formally trained.

And why should she be trained?

To protect herself. Someone is out to manipulate the judges.

The Heragi Empire?

We don't know for sure who — yet.

Synthia nodded and took in her garden setting and beloved cicichimp. Then she closed her eyes. I knew she was thinking about coming with me or not. I did not invade her thoughts. And I probably couldn't if I tried.

I don't feel Stoller is dead, she thought to me.

"What?" I said out loud.

"You heard what I said. But we can talk like this if you are more comfortable. I don't feel he has left this dimension."

"I saw his skiff blow up. He was on it."

"Was he?" she asked.

I thought back to the explosion and Kron's ship taking off into hyperdrive.

I stood up.

"Let me pack a bag." Synthia said as she headed inside. Her cicichimp stared at me and chirped. I chirped back. Then the little pet followed Synthia into her home.

We took the next waterhover to the planet-port, and we were soon on the *Alyssia* — me, Synthia and her cicichimp Greena.

"Hello, Synthia," said Feti as we boarded.

"Hello, Feti. This is my friend Greena."

"Welcome, Greena."

"Synthia believes Stoller may be alive."

"That is excellent news," said Feti. "But how is that?"

"He may have been on Kron's ship when the skiff was hit."

"That is a possibility. I didn't do a bio-metric scan of the skiff or Kron's ship when it left. So the justices' consciousnesses are safe," said Feti.

"Consciousnesses?" inquired Synthia.

"They were extracted and copies made when they had their transfer operation."

"That's not good," she said.

"Why?" I asked.

"A person can't have two consciousnesses in one dimension. One or the other will ascend or descend to another dimension."

"And what will happen exactly?"

"One or the other will disappear," said Synthia.

"Disappear?" I said. "You mean die?"

"No, not die. One will disappear from this dimension that you and I are experiencing and go to a different one that we are not a part of," explained Synthia.

I surveyed the Karakova Highway and watched the streams of light pass by us. Disappear?

"How do you stop that from happening? The disappearing," I asked.

"Either you don't or one has to be destroyed," said Synthia.

"Oh, dear," said Feti.

Indeed, I thought.

We were nearing the exit to Zaradorba. I steered us off the highway and resumed our course to get back to the Kells' lab as soon as possible.

I decided to carry Synthia and Greena as we left the *Alyssia* for the Kells' lab on Zaradorba. I didn't want to slowly walk Synthia's pace with the information we had. Feti sent a message to the team to have them assemble at the medbay lab.

I kicked the lab doors open with Synthia in my arms. Zara gasped with surprise. I put Synthia and Greena down.

"Synthia!" Zara ran up to hug her old friend.

"Zara," said Synthia.

I scanned the room, and there at a table was a card game in mid-play. It was Stoller's quinker cards. Goggins was engaged in the game as were Ava and Damiel Kell.

The lab door burst open and Stoller appeared, explaining quinker rules to the three justices.

"Stoller!" I ran up to him and reeled him around in the air.

"Oomph! Gabe! Whoa there," he said as he patted me on the shoulder. I realized I'd made a pretty human response just then. But I didn't care too much.

Stoller was alive.

Everyone in the room jumped up. Laughter and grunts filled the room.

I put Stoller down.

"What happened?" I asked.

"Kron is what happened. He sent the skiff out as a decoy. He was right too. Look," said Stoller as he pointed to the three justices' floating consciousness spheres in a glass jar near the Kells. "Like I told you, me and Kron have a bond. It isn't a pretty bond, but it's a bond all the same."

"They're still here. All of you are," I said, changing my attention from the floating spheres to the three justices standing before me. Guy, Tefara and Lilou tilted their heads as they stared at me.

"Yes, of course we are," said Lilou as she stepped forward.

"What's wrong, Gabe?" asked Ava.

"And why did you bring Synthia? Not that I don't love seeing you," said Goggins with a nod to her.

"I've missed you, too," Synthia said with grin.

"Do you want to explain?" I asked Synthia.

"Yes," she said. "Please, everyone, sit."

Everyone gathered around the lab table. "Guy, Tefara, Lilou, this is Synthia. She's a telepath and a teacher in the ancient ways. She has helped us in the past."

"I know of her," said Lilou.

Synthia nodded. I was sure Anjori had told Lilou about her.

Synthia rose and began to speak. "Hundreds of years ago, my people also experimented with consciousness operations, and we stopped because of the consequences. We found that a person can't have two consciousnesses in one dimension. One will undoubtedly disappear."

"What?" said Goggins. "But look, they are both here."

"Yes, for now. But within fourteen sols, one or the other will not be on our dimension."

Goggins laughed and shook his head in disbelief. "So, this

happened to your people, but how do we know it will happen to us? Here?"

"All I can tell you is what we experienced. There will be signs, but they will be fast, then it will be too late."

"What are the signs?" asked Damiel.

"Pain in the person's mind as they are splitting. The Kells may be able to monitor pain sensors on the consciousness spheres. And then they will simply vanish," said Synthia.

"That's crazy," said Goggins.

"Maybe not," said Guy. "I've been getting headaches. I shared that with the Kells this morning."

Tefara spoke up. "I must say that I also have had headaches. I thought it was the stress."

"Lilou?" I asked.

"No, none," she said.

"One or the other must stay alive. But not both," said Synthia with care.

"I'm sorry," said Goggins, lowering his head. Zara rubbed his back.

The justices were somber.

"So we will move forward with the surgeries," said Ava. "We have no margin for error. There will be no back up. We will save all the good code we can from your robotic bodies, wipe clean your CPUs and then upload the consciousness spheres."

"Piece of cake," said Stoller, trying to lift the mood. It didn't.

"What about the memories we gained while we have been robots?" asked Guy.

"They will be wiped. Gone," said Damiel.

"No. I don't want that. I don't want to forget," said Guy.

"Me either," said Tefara.

"I have to admit, I don't want that either," said Lilou.

"We need to fight the virus that is inside you," said Damiel. "With a total clean wipe of your code, we can start over."

"I don't want to start over," said Guy.

Damiel stood up. He was frustrated. He wanted to help the justices, but the whole situation had limitations.

Zara spoke up. "We can decipher all the new code in their CPUs that was made immediately after the surgery was completed. Load that to a separate drive. Then scan for viruses."

"There's still a chance of infection. If the scan doesn't catch all of the virus."

"I'm willing to take that chance," said Guy.

"Me too," said Tefara.

"Yes, I will too," said Lilou.

"But this decision may be bigger than you. We have to think of the galaxy. If you get latent effects, you will go crazy."

"We will demand that the Galactic Council have you and Ava monitor us," said Tefara.

"Maybe being immortal is not all that great," said Guy. "And when it is our time, if that comes about, then so be it. But we *are* our memories."

Ava stood up. "Then it's time to get to work. We respect your wishes."

The Kells, Goggins and Zara began discussing the details of the upcoming surgery.

Stoller began a card game with Guy and Tefara. I leaned over to Lilou and asked her to follow me. I led her over to Synthia and introduced them.

I put them together, and then I closed my eyes and went into my mind. I made the cube that Synthia taught me to do to aid in a concentrated telepathic conversation where no one could break into my mind. Into my cube, I brought Synthia and Lilou. At first, Lilou was frightened. She searched inside my cube as if she were trying to escape.

I then sent them both a thought. *Lilou, don't be frightened. You are in my mind. I want to introduce you to Synthia.*

Synthia reached out her hand. Lilou poked at it to see if it was real.

Go ahead, it will feel real. And who are we to say it is not? thought Synthia, and then she laughed.

Lilou shook Synthia's hand and thought, *Nice to meet you.*

Very good, thought Synthia. *Gabe told me of your gift.*

I hid it for a very long time, thought Lilou.

Yes, you must have. He tells me you are part Heragi.

Yes.

Right, hence the gift.

I want Synthia to teach you, Lilou, I thought. *She can show you many things.*

Why?

To protect yourself. It may be useful one day, I thought.

Lilou nodded. *Okay, thank you.*

My pleasure.

When do we begin? asked Lilou.

Now, thought Synthia. *Come inside my mind. Gabe, you may leave us.*

Of course, I thought.

I dissolved my mind's cube and opened my eyes. Stoller pulled out a chair next to him. "Have a seat," he said to me. "I'll deal you in."

"Thanks." I sat down. "You're at a disadvantage."

Stoller looked at Guy, Tefara and me, all robots, playing quinker with him.

"I like a challenge," said Stoller with a wink.

We played for many hours before the Kells, Goggins and Zara were ready for us. Or really, ready for the justices and their surgery.

16

The justices' consciousness spheres hovered and moved across the glass container in the Kells' lab. I watched them change colors with small pulses every few moments. From looking at the spheres, there was no way of knowing which consciousness belonged to which justice.

Synthia came up to me.

"How did the training go with Lilou?"

"Excellent. She's a quick study and was able to accelerate her learning. She can now fortify her mind," she said.

"Good. Thank you."

"You're welcome."

"Your planet stopped transferring consciousnesses into robots?"

"We weren't trying to put them into robots. We were trying to put them in other things — plants, animals, young people. They were misguided, our ancestors. Then they perfected the ancient ways such as telepathy, and they left immortality to the other higher dimensions."

"So what we are doing is wrong?"

"No. Every civilization needs to walk their path."

"What or who is in the higher dimensions?"

"Those whose reality is an octave or two higher. Some say a higher intelligence or the creators of all the dimensions."

"A higher intelligence? I wonder if robots are there."

Synthia smiled. "I don't know. One day, perhaps, we will find out."

Ava walked up to greet us. "Hello. We're ready to begin."

"Good luck," said Synthia as she took a seat in the back of the lab.

"Gabe, thank you for retrieving the consciousnesses. We are always putting you in dangerous situations."

"That is why I was created. Right?"

Ava lowered her head. I shouldn't have answered her that way. I didn't want her to feel guilty. She created me, and I should always be grateful for that. She and Damiel gave me life.

"I'm happy to help. I always am," I said. She looked up, and I saw pain in her eyes. My chest hurt.

"Maybe after all of this, we can spend some time together. I'd like to know all that you have seen and learned since Heragi."

"I can send you a report."

"No, I don't want a report." She touched my shoulder. "I want to talk with you. Like we used to in the lab."

I remembered those times in the lab. Every day, Ava and Damiel were teaching me things. Now, I was supposed to teach her and Damiel.

I nodded. "Okay. I'd be happy to do that."

"Good," she said.

I turned to leave her so she could prepare for the surgery. I then turned back to face her. "I miss you."

"I miss you, too," she said. And then she smiled. I hadn't seen her smile like that for a long time. A warmth hit my chest. I went to the justices' sides who were on their gurneys being prepped for surgery by Zara and Goggins. I bid them good luck.

Lilou turned to me. "Gabe."

I went to her. "I hear you are a very good student."

"Synthia has been very patient with me," she said. "Gabe, if anything happens, I want you to go to Anjori and tell her everything."

"I will," I said. "But I don't believe that will be needed. You're in good hands."

"I wish you could see me smile," she said. "I am smiling."

I touched her face. "I know," I said. "Me too."

Stoller entered the lab and took a seat. I sat down next to him to observe the surgery. Stoller leaned over to me. "So, you were pretty choked up when you thought I was a goner, huh?" he said with a smirk.

"I was also upset that we lost the skiff," I retorted.

He stifled a laugh. "Gabe, after the surgery, if it's a success, we need the justices to send a video to the Galactic Council."

"To say what?" I asked.

"To give them the news. Someone messed with their code, and we are all innocent. Right now, we are the most wanted people and robot in the galaxy. It's only a matter of time before they figure out we're on Zaradorba."

"Copy that," I said.

"This galaxy is getting too small. After this, I wouldn't mind a nice long vacation in the Edge," he said.

"What do you do on a vacation?" I asked.

"It's not really much different than what I do now. Except I don't have three different military naval units chasing after me."

"I guess having the Heragi, Rothworth and the Galactic Council's military searching for us isn't exactly a respite, is it?"

"No, it's not. Maybe one or two planets after us but not two plus the whole galaxy. Since I started hanging out with you, you've upped the adrenaline in my life."

"And vice versa," I said.

Stoller laughed and said, "That's why we get along."

Zara shot us a glance. "Shhh."

Goggins whispered, "We're beginning."

Stoller gave them both a thumbs up.

The justices were again connected to Damiel and Ava's computer systems and monitors.

"They're ready," said Ava.

"Copy that," said Zara as she began her lightning speed coding.

"Beginning their download," said Goggins as he and Zara began downloading the justices' new experiences since their last surgery.

"Connecting the electrodes to the spheres for remote download," said Damiel as he implanted the devices into the consciousnesses. Ava began her coding work on the spheres.

Zara and Goggins carefully reviewed the justices' old code and scrubbed it for any trace of the virus.

Ava reviewed the interpretation of the consciousness cells into the code that would soon be transferred into the justices.

I glanced over to Synthia. She had her eyes closed. She was in meditation, and although I didn't try to eavesdrop into her mind to see what she was doing, I was sure she was holding a safe space in her mind for the justices to feel well during the surgery.

"Why do they want to live forever?" whispered Stoller to me.

"They want to serve the galaxy," I whispered back.

"No offense, but I wouldn't want to be immortal."

"No offense taken. I wouldn't want you to be immortal either," I said.

Stoller laughed and got a quick leveling stare from Zara. He held up his hands in defense.

. . .

Hours went by before Ava and Damiel turned from the operating tables. "We've completed the procedures," said Damiel. I nudged Stoller, who had fallen asleep. Synthia opened her eyes from her meditation.

Goggins and Zara did a high-five. "We believe we uploaded and downloaded all their new code virus-free," said Goggins.

We approached the justices.

"Lilou, please open your eyes," said Ava.

Her blue eyes opened, and she turned her head toward Ava. "Dr. Kell, was it a success?"

"Yes, Lilou. We believe it was," said Ava.

Damiel woke Guy and Tefara. Goggins and Zara began testing their cognitive and memory recall.

I was about to walk up to Damiel and Ava to congratulate them when Feti broke in over my arm comm. "Gabe? We have a situation."

"What is it, Feti?" I asked.

"We have two Rothworth naval ships entering the Zaradorba atmosphere."

Stoller headed for the door and shouted, "Gabe, I'm going to the *Alyssia*."

"Prepare for launch, Feti," I said.

"Copy that," said Feti.

"Ava, Damiel," I said. "We need to have the justices prepare a video message for the Galactic Council. They need to explain what has happened with your help. Can you do that?"

"Of course," said Damiel.

"We need it done now. And have them call off Rothworth's ships. Stoller and I will try to hold them off," I said.

"Gabe, we were able to decipher who implanted the Heragi prime directive," said Goggins as he stepped forward.

"Who was it?" I asked.

"It had the imprint from Dr. Julipo's computers back on the

Justice Station. I was the last one who would want to admit that, but it's true."

The justices shook their heads.

"How could he?" said Tefara.

"We trusted him with our lives," said Guy.

"And the virus?" I asked.

"Rothworth," said Zara as she stood up. "We traced it back to a key coding imprint from his planet, and we found the time-stamp he overlooked. It was implanted the evening he checked the justices' code after the dinner party."

"But why?" asked Lilou

"We can only surmise that he wanted the virus to be detected and to have Ameribot Industries blamed, so he could gain full control of the contract for your rebuild or future robot manufac-turing. Whether he had good or bad intentions, we don't know for sure. But it was malicious."

"Or Jessio did it to control us at a future date," said Lilou.

I started for the door. "We need that message to the Galactic Council immediately."

"Copy that," said Goggins.

I turned around. "Alert the rebel base leader here on Zaradorba that we have hostile ships if they don't know that already. And where is Jebediah?"

"We contacted him yesterday. He's on his way back from the Edge," said Damiel.

Stoller and Feti had the *Alyssia* ready for departure from Zaradorba as I ran up the ramp. I strapped into the commander seat, and we lifted off. Feti gave coordinates on where to find the two Rothworth naval ships. As we came out of Zaradorba's atmosphere into space, we could see the two ships.

"Feti, please set up a comm link with that Rothworth destroyer," I said.

"Copy that. One moment please," said Feti. "Go ahead, Gabe."

"This is the commander of the *Alyssia*. Who am I speaking with?" I asked.

"This is Jessio Rothworth. Hello, Gabe."

"Jessio, I'm asking you to stand down."

"Where are the justices?" he demanded.

"They are safe."

"You were meeting a bounty hunter who stole their consciousnesses out of the Justice Station lab," he said.

"And you fired upon and destroyed my skiff," I replied.

The other naval vessel was trying to flank us. I skirted back to give us more room and try to draw both naval ships away from Zaradorba.

"We know what you did, Jessio," I said.

There was silence on his end.

Feti turned off the comm to speak to us. "Gabe, there is a broadcast being sent out to the Galactic Council from Zaradorba. I've been asked to relay it to any nearby comm substations."

"Will they see it on the two naval ships?" asked Stoller.

"Affirmative, I can send it to any ship in our vicinity," said Feti.

"Then do it," I said.

The video came on all of our monitors. Jessio would be seeing it also. The video showed the three justices sitting all together. Lilou was in the middle and began to speak. "My fellow Zephon galactic citizens and the distinguished Galactic Council, this is Supreme Court Justice Lilou Prado, Justice Tefara Kimathi and Justice Guy Cadiux. We are sending you this message of our own accord. We are healthy and safe."

Stoller leaned over toward me. "Is she going to out Jessio?"

"I certainly hope so," I said.

"Yeah, me too. That blasted rich boy almost killed me," said Stoller.

We continued to listen to Lilou. "We left the Justice Station under duress that someone may have tampered with our code, and that was a correct assumption. We had our code reviewed by an independent third party that confirmed rogue code was implanted by Dr. Julipo on behalf of the Heragi Empire. And that a coded virus was also inserted by Jessio Rothworth."

We watched as the Rothworth naval ships began to pull back away from Zaradorba.

"Look at them run," said Stoller.

Lilou continued, "My fellow galaxy constituents, please call off any naval vessels in the area of Zaradorba. We are here on this planet getting medical and technical treatment and will soon be leaving to go back to the Justice Station. We owe our lives to the professional assistance of friends to our galaxy, not enemies. I will be communicating privately with the directors of the Galactic Council later this sol, but we wanted all parties to be aware of the betrayal that was made against us and our galaxy's citizens. Peace be within our galaxy."

And with that, the video ended.

"There you have it. The Heragi Empire and the Rothworth Dynasty are in a ton of hot water now," Stoller said as he whipped around in his chair. "And it couldn't have happened to a nicer bunch of folks, right?"

"Gabe, we have an incoming comm from General Jebediah Kell," said Feti.

"Uh oh," said Stoller. "He's not going to be happy."

"Why is that?" I asked before I opened up the comm to Jeb.

"We basically led two naval warships to his rebel planet. What do you think?"

"Yeah, you have a point," I said. "Feti, go ahead and open the comm."

"Gabe?" It was Jeb.

"Yes, Jebediah?"

"What in blazes do you and Stoller think you're doing? Are

you crazy?" yelled Jeb. "Zaradorba is not some type of pit stop for all your galaxy bar fights."

"Bar fights?" said an indignant Stoller. "Jeb, we just saved the galactic Supreme Court justices."

"Yes, that's good. Really, I'm glad for that. But, frazzle me. It's just that Zaradorba is vulnerable."

I held up my hands to Stoller to stop him from talking. I knew I could calm down Jeb. He was just worried about his people.

"I'm sorry. We needed Damiel and Ava to help us. They were the only ones we could turn to. We'll get ahold of you first if we ever need to come down to Zaradorba again."

"Thank you, Gabe," said Jeb.

"I'll just bring the *Alyssia* down to pick up the justices, Zara and Goggins, and we'll be on our way," I said.

"No, let me go pick them up and return them to you," said Jeb.

The comm went dead.

"He hung up," said Feti. "Is General Kell perturbed with us?"

"Yes," I said.

"But then again, what's new? He's always mad at us," said Stoller. "Geez, he won't even let us go back down to pick up our crew."

"There is some type of protocol we should keep — even with rebels," I said.

Jebediah returned and docked into our port entrance to deliver the justices, Zara and Goggins. I greeted them as they boarded.

Zara and Goggins came aboard first.

"Gabe, hello, always nice to be back on the *Alyssia*," said Goggins.

"Nice work keeping Jessio away," said Zara.

Then the three justices boarded.

"Hello, Gabe," said Guy. "Thank you for taking us back to the Justice Station."

"My pleasure," I said.

"Yes, thank you," said Tefara.

Lilou boarded, and Damiel and Ava Kell followed her in.

"The Kells are coming with us back to the Justice Station," said Lilou. "We'll need them to explain the details to the directors of the Galactic Council."

"Does Jeb know?" I asked.

"Yes, and he's escorting the *Alyssia* with his own ship," said Damiel.

"I think he wanted us all to have a bit more protection," said Ava as she passed by me.

As I returned to the bridge, I viewed Jeb's ship, the *Otessis,* ahead of us. He definitely wanted to lead us in.

"What's he doing?" asked a suspicious Stoller, pointing at Jeb's ship.

"He's our escort," I said.

Stoller rolled his eyes. "Escort? Fine. The more the merrier. It will be like old times."

All our passengers settled in. I glanced back at the justices, and they seemed fine, but I had nothing to compare that too. I'd check on them later. Specifically, I would check in with Lilou later.

I started our engines and followed Jebediah out of the area and toward the Justice Station.

17

———

I put the pilot controls on automatic with Feti overseeing. Damiel asked that everyone go down to the galley for a meeting. I assumed he wanted to give an update on the condition of the justices.

I was the last one to the room and decided to stand next to the window where Zara was standing.

"Hey, Gabe," said Zara.

"Hello," I said.

"I see Jebediah was in his usual mood," she said.

"He wasn't happy we came to Zaradorba, but that's water under the bridge now"

"Is it?" she said with a smile.

"I hope so," I said.

Damiel stood up and began his meeting. "Thanks everyone for joining us. Let me get Jeb with us." He went over to the wall comm. "Feti, can you connect us with Jeb?"

"Yes, Dr. Kell. One moment," said Feti. "He's on."

Damiel typed on the wall comm and threw the hologram comm link of Jeb in the middle of the table. "Hey, Jeb."

"Hello, everyone."

"We wanted to discuss our upcoming docking at the Justice Station," said Damiel. "Go ahead, Jeb."

"I wanted to review some logistics that are in play. We are all very happy that the justices are healthy and that you helped to uncover what the Heragi Empire and the Rothworth Dynasty had done to their code."

"*But*—" said Stoller as he folded his arms against his chest.

"*And* there are some logistics that we need to explain that are in play," finished Jeb.

"Listen, Jeb, just tell us what's going on. What did we mess up? If that is what you're referring to," said Zara.

Stoller stared back at Zara and nodded. He obviously approved of Zara's straight talk with Jeb. I wasn't sure if he knew that Zara and Jeb had become close during our last fire fight with the Heragi Empire when we were on Zaradorba the first time. I could fill him in on that later. Or Zara could.

"Okay. This is how it seems to be playing out. When Lilou made her galactic-wide video accusing the Heragi Empire of tampering with their code —" said Jeb before being interrupted by Goggins.

"They did!"

"Yes, they may have or did do that, but they are now on red alert, and many think they will withdraw from the Galactic Council," explained Jeb.

"So what?" said Stoller.

"The Galactic Council is holding the civility of this galaxy together," said Jeb.

"They didn't help you much, if at all, when the Heragi Empire court-martialed you and were about to throw you in prison for life and also throw your own brother and sister-in-law in prison. And who knows what they will do? And they have tried, haven't they? With your nephew and nieces for having the ancient gifts," spewed out Stoller, who got up from his chair in a heated moment.

"That's enough. I'm very aware of the Heragi Empire and the evil they are capable of doing."

"Then stop being a diplomat and start being the warrior you are," yelled Stoller.

"You are the last one who should be lecturing me on being a warrior, you washed-up pilot," said Jeb.

"Gentlemen, gentlemen," said Lilou, standing up. Everyone quieted. Only a person with Lilou's status could quiet such large personalities as Jeb and Stoller's. She strode around the room. "What Jebediah Kell is warning of is important. I felt it was the right thing to do, to warn the galaxy of what the Heragis and Rothworths did to us. And we needed them to know that Gabe, his crew and the Kells were on the right side of the galaxy. But things are complicated now."

Stoller raised his hands. "Things in our galaxy have always been complicated, at least in my lifetime. So now we know which side people are on."

"The Galactic Council is splintering, Stoller," said Jeb.

"So let it splinter," yelled Stoller.

"It means war, death. Thousands if not millions could be hurt," said Jeb.

"They are already hurting, it's just a slower death," said Stoller as spun a chair out of his way. "Listen, I'm not a politician. But we were trying to find allies to help us fight against the Heragi Empire. So this has only helped us. We know who is on our side now." And then he left the room.

"He may be right," said Ava.

"Diplomacy must always be tried first," said Jeb.

The room was silent.

"There is a Galactic Council meeting coordinated for when we return. We will be asked to present all the facts and updates in regard to the justices' health and well-being. They will want to understand what exactly happened. We are all expected to attend," said Damiel.

"That is all we wanted to relay," said Jeb. "We will be there soon. Over and out." And then the hologram screen went down.

I didn't know exactly what to think or say. Perhaps we started the splintering of the Galactic Council as Jeb said, but we didn't plant the rogue code — that was the Heragis. And we didn't plant the virus in the justices — that was Jessio Rothworth. We were only trying to help. What was done was done. I started for the door to go back to the bridge.

"Gabe," said Lilou. She grabbed my arm to pull me back to talk. "We don't blame you. I wanted you to know. We're grateful."

I nodded. "There's no going backward."

"There never is," said Lilou.

"Is the Galactic Council strong? Do you trust those that sit on the Council?"

"There are good directors on the Council, there are politicians on the Council and there are weak directors on the Council. For the most part, they have all pulled together when needed. But we will see who lives in fear and who lives more for the future benefit of all, not just their planet," she said.

"I'm like Stoller. I'm just a pilot," I said.

"You're more than that," said Lilou as she held my hand.

Ava was watching us. I pulled my hand gently away from Lilou. She was human and robot, but she was a galactic Supreme Court justice, and her safety was my first concern. My second concern was that she was prepared to be a robot for the rest of her life. I still didn't know if she understood what that meant.

"We're approaching the Justice Station. I need to get to the bridge," I said.

"Of course," said Lilou.

I left the galley. Lilou reaching out to me had startled me. And having Ava look at Lilou holding my hand had somehow made me feel guilt. I needed time to process this new feeling Lilou had sparked in me.

. . .

When I arrived on the bridge, Stoller was still hot under the collar from what Jeb inferred at the meeting. At least from Stoller's interpretation of that Jeb inferred.

"Did I sound like a buffoon?" asked Stoller.

"Since when are you worried about what other people think of you?" I asked.

"I'm not, not at all."

We both went back to enjoying the view of the Karakova Highway. I followed Jeb's ship that was exiting for the final stretch to the Justice Station.

"I don't like war. I'm not asking for it," said Stoller.

"We all know that," I said. "Jeb is trying to say to tread softly."

"Do you think that will work?" he asked.

"No, but one should first try. Let's see what mood the Galactic Council is in," I said.

"We're not walking into a trap, are we?"

"We will soon know." I snuck a peek over to Stoller. He smirked and rubbed his chin. I guessed what he really was asking was what was the likelihood we would be thrown into jail. Or the likelihood that he would be thrown into jail — again. Stoller wouldn't be able to handle that, I could tell. He thrived on freedom, and I didn't believe any jail cell would contain him again. He would see to that — one way or another.

I decided I needed to especially keep an eye on Stoller in the meeting with the Galactic Council directors. I read that trapped animals are at their most dangerous when first contained. But I thought Stoller would be the most dangerous after a second attempted containment — it just wasn't going to happen again.

"Gabe, we are within comms of the Justice Station. And a visual of the station will be attainable in a few seconds."

"Thank you, Feti."

Goggins and Zara came up to the bridge and took their seats.

"Welcome," I said to them, and I meant it. Having the crew on the bridge, our bridge, was something I'd missed and hadn't known it until right then.

"Thank you," said Zara. "It's much less stressful here than in an operating room."

"Yes, having that much responsibility for a Supreme Court justice's life isn't something I want to experience again," said Goggins.

"How are the justices?" I asked. "Have there been any issues since the surgery?"

"No issues. At least nothing has appeared. We also have to trust that they would tell us if they were not feeling normal," said Zara.

"What is normal for them? I can't imagine making that adjustment," said Stoller.

"Yes, it was an extraordinary choice they made to become robots," said Goggins.

"If we missed any part or strand of the virus, it will duplicate and can be identified," said Zara.

Stoller turned around. "But what do you think of their choice to become robots? You haven't expressed your opinion. Are you for it or against it?"

"I'm not for it or against it. It was their choice. They made it," Zara answered flatly.

"Would you do it?" he asked.

Zara paused. "No. Unless —"

"Unless what?" Stoller pressed.

"I had someone to spend eternity with. Or who would outlive me. Or whose parts would outlast mine."

"How would that be any different from how humans or aliens live today? You have no guarantees on who, whether friends, partners, or colleagues, will outlast you," I said.

"Wow, very wise for a robot," said Goggins. "When do you think of all this? When we're sleeping?"

"There is much time to kill when everyone is sleeping. That was one of the issues the justices need or needed to work out," I said.

"Did you tell them what you do?" asked Zara.

"Yes," I said.

"And that's why you taught them quinker, correct?" asked Stoller with a smile.

Goggins and Zara laughed.

"Yes, the card game that gives you hours and hours of entertainment," said Goggins.

"Especially if someone is dribbling out the rules every time you play. It takes a lifetime to learn," she said.

"True, there is a lot to learn with the game. But, overall, I think quinker teaches us all something," said Stoller.

"What in the stars would that be?" asked Goggins.

"Patience," said Stoller.

Goggins and Zara howled at Stoller's stoic answer.

"While liquidating all your galaxy credits," added Zara.

"And frustrating you to the point of madness," said Goggins.

"However you interpret it," said Stoller as he winked at me. "If it still frustrates you, then you haven't learned its lesson yet."

"Gabe, the Justice Station has given us clearance to dock the *Alyssia*. Please proceed to gate 671," said Feti.

"Thank you," I said.

We pulled into the enclosed docking port and exited the ship with the others. We met Jebediah inside the Justice Station on the main floor and were immediately ushered by Galactic Council police to a conference room at the top of the Justice Station next to the Supreme Court room.

It was the conference room for the Galactic Council. All of

the directors had assembled in-person, which was quite rare according to Lilou.

Stoller had been jittery since we left the *Alyssia*. He touched the weapon hidden under his coat multiple times as the GC police escorted us up the multitude of escalators.

"Easy, Stoller," I had said to him a few times on the ride up to the top.

"I'm fine," he said, but he wasn't anywhere near fine as I scanned his bio-metrics. His nervous system metrics were rising although he had a cool exterior. I needed to count on Stoller not babysit him. *I hope the GC police don't try anything stupid.*

Synthia was walking behind me and sent me a thought. *I'll watch him too.*

There I go thinking out loud again. I was fine if Synthia was tuned into my thoughts. But I didn't want Lilou to be reviewing my thoughts. I should ask Synthia if she taught Lilou some dos and don'ts of telepathy. I assumed so. I hoped so.

We were waiting to be invited inside the director's conference room when Jeb headed over to me.

"Gabe," he said in a whisper. "Are you keeping a watch on Stoller?"

"Yes," I said.

"Good. Me too."

"We're all on the same side," I reminded him.

"I know we are," he said. "Listen, if things go sideways, we have permission to go to the Oliveria Providence."

"You talked with Anjori?" I asked.

"Yes, she understands the situation."

"Where are your nephew and nieces?" I asked. The last I heard, the Kell children were doing reconnaissance near Heragi to see if they could assist any others who had the ancient gifts and were being watched by the Heragi Empire.

"I contacted them yesterday. They're on their way here, upon my instruction, to meet us at Oliveria."

"Copy that," I said.

The three justices were calmly sitting and chatting amongst themselves. It was really their story to tell since they paid the ultimate sacrifice. But the justices were raised and educated on how laws may or may not be interpreted. They couldn't give much counsel on when to wage war and upon whom, and I wasn't sure they wanted to do that.

I glanced over to the Kells, Damiel and Ava. They were talking with Goggins and Zara. Most likely, they were reviewing the technical explanation they would give to the non-technical directors. Ava caught my eye. She smiled at me.

When would we all be gathered like this again? A pain went through my chest.

One of the GC police came out of the conference room and made an announcement. "You may all now enter." Everyone filed in and took seats at a large circular desk. One of the directors, an avian species, began first, "Welcome back, Lilou, Tefara and Guy. We were very pleased to hear that you were safe when we received your video message. How are you all feeling?"

"Thank you, Theron. We are feeling healthy, now, with the help of our friends," Lilou said with a nod to the Kells, Goggins and Zara.

"Thank you also to everyone else in attendance. We have studied background information on all of you, and you are an eclectic bunch, to say the least, but we have no ill will toward any of you. We are grateful for each one of you and the part you may have played," said an older human-looking director.

"Thank you. I'm Jebediah Kell. Some of us are wanted by the Heragi Empire, and we are coming here under a bit of trepidation, but we want the best for the galaxy and this Galactic Council. We take no pleasure in accusations, even if they are credible."

"Thank you," said an alien director. "I would like to hear

from the Kells on the coding and health discoveries they identified with the justices."

Ava and Damiel rose, and from their arm comms, they threw holograms into the air with the coding information that identified the Heragi Empire and the Rothworth Dynasty tracing. They explained the prime directive and virus coding they found and how it traced back to the two planets in question.

"Thank you, Ava and Damiel," said Theron. "These are very grave concerns. And we have decided to enforce sanctions on both the Heragi and the Rothworth solar system. They will not be happy, but it is a necessary discipline."

"Shouldn't you hear from their leaders?" asked Guy. "To hear their side of the story?"

"As you know, this is not a court, Guy. We don't need one to hand down sanctions," said the avian director.

"The atrocity is self-evident with the proof that has been thus far provided. We have already discussed the sanctions with both planets," said Theron.

"And?" said Stoller. I poked him in the ribs. Really, he didn't have to speak. He shoved me back. Classy.

"And they have both broken from the Council. They informed us of that right before you walked in," said another director.

"What does this mean? Exactly?" asked Jeb.

"There have been no formal war declarations," said Theron. "The Galactic Council has been fractured but not totally split apart. We will continue on with our galactic courts and monitor Heragi and Rothworth."

"So, what? Everybody is on their own against those two planets?" asked Stoller as he rose from his chair, undoubtedly to get away from another rib knock from me.

"Yes, for the time being. The Galactic Council Police will protect the Justice Station, the directors and the Supreme Court justices, but we will have to lean on the alliance that we heard

Jebediah Kell was forming. What do you call it?" asked the avian director.

"The Federation of Free Planets," said Jebediah.

Goggins leaned over to me and Zara. "Was that the name we settled on? Egads, that's a mouthful."

"Yes, I remember we had drinks at the Blue Edger bar on Charbeaux Station. Darn, I miss that bar."

"Shhh," said Zara to both of them.

I laughed a small grunt, and everyone looked at me. I pretended to cough. But how many robots need to cough? None.

"Yes, the FFP," said Theron as he pointed to Jebediah. "We have limited resources, and we are not a planet, just a governing body trying to hold the galactic parties accountable. The planets have the resources, we have the laws."

"Jebediah, we would like you to lead the effort to unite the galaxy, as it once was," said the other alien director.

Jeb laughed and shook his head. "That was our intent. But I confess, that may be next to impossible."

"Damiel and Ava, are the three justices healthy enough to resume their duties in court?" asked Theron.

"Yes," said Damiel.

"We would like the Kells to be our only monitoring scientists. We trust them," said Guy as he stood.

"We will grant this request," said the avian director.

"Thank you," said Guy as he sat down and clenched hands with Lilou and Tefara. I was glad that made them feel good. They would need it. And Ava could continue to counsel them. The transition or adjustment for them was just in its infancy. I knew that, and Ava knew that also.

"I actually agree with him for once," Stoller whispered to me. I nudged him again with my arm in his ribs.

"Try, that is all we ask," said Theron. "Thank you all."

And with that, we were dismissed, and we left the conference room.

Outside in the hallway, Jeb came up to Stoller and me. "We need to leave immediately." He also grabbed Ava and Damiel to come close in to him. "I heard from Alex. They are in the middle of a fight right now."

"Between who?" asked Ava. There was panic in her voice.

"Heragi's Foxwell and Rothworth," said Jeb. "Let's go."

I sent Lilou a thought. *Goodbye.*

She thought back, *Be safe.*

Damiel, Ava and Synthia stayed on the Justice Station with the justices. Jeb took command of his ship, and Stoller, Goggins and Zara headed to the *Alyssia* for a fast launch from the Justice Station.

18

———

We strapped into our chairs on the *Alyssia* and followed Jeb's ship, the *Otessis*, away from the Justice Station.

"Goggins, do you have the location of Alex Kell's ship?" I asked.

"Do you mean *my* ship?" asked Stoller. "I only leant it to Alex and his sisters."

"He's probably taking better care of the *Ravena* than you did," said Zara.

"We're on the right track. Five hundred more miles," said Goggins as he reviewed his monitor.

"Feti, please set up a comm link to the *Ravena* when they are in range, and add in Jebediah," I said.

"Copy that," said Feti.

"Going to the gun turret," said Stoller as he left the bridge.

"Gabe, coming up on our starboard. We have the two naval ships. General Foxwell's Heragi ship *Firestone* and Jessio Roth-worth's naval ship called the *Sundra*. And I think I've located the *Ravena*, too," said Goggins.

I turned on my comm. "Jeb?"

"Yeah, Gabe, I copy you," he said.

"We have a visual on the ships," I said.

"Copy that. Let's see what's going on," said Jeb.

"Gabe, General Kell, we have a comm link to Alex," said Feti.

"Copy that," said Jeb. "Alex?"

"Hey, Uncle Jeb. Hi, Gabe. Boy, it's good to see you," said Alex.

"Hi there," said Honora.

"Hello," said Talia's responder.

It was good to hear from all the Kell children. My heart warmed and then that was replaced with an ache as I saw that Foxwell's *Firestone* ship was towing the *Ravena* which the children were on.

"Is that a tow line?" I asked.

"Copy that," said Goggins.

The *Sundra* was circling the *Ravena* like it was preparing to attack.

"Jeb, what's your assessment?" I asked.

"We need to get a comm link to both of the commanders, Jessio and Foxwell," said Jeb.

"There you go with diplomacy first," said Stoller from the gun turret.

"You need to shut it," yelled Jeb. "I'm trying to save my nephew and nieces."

"They're on the comm link," I reminded Jeb.

"Sorry, kids. Stoller seems to get the best of me sometimes," said Jeb.

"Yeah, sorry kids. We just want you safe," apologized Stoller.

Zara leaned over and whispered to me, "Just like old times."

"True," I said. "Feti, open up a link to the *Firestone* and the *Sundra*."

"Copy that, Gabe," said Feti. After a few moments, Feti got back to us. "We have General Foxwell and Jessio Rothworth, Gabe."

"Go ahead, Jeb," I said.

"Foxwell, Jessio, this is Jebediah Kell. Foxwell, we need you to release the *Ravena* right now."

"Afraid that's not possible. I'm taking the children back to Heragi for questioning. They were caught hacking into our defense ministry files, and they are practicing telepathy which has been banned in the Heragi Empire," said Foxwell.

"Right, I remember how you kidnapped Honora and Talia and tried to use their powers to reveal rebels fighting against your empire. You're so full of it, General," said Jeb.

I started pulling around to flank General Foxwell's ship.

"Jessio, I could use some assistance," said Jeb.

"Help you? We tried to help the justices, but we were sanctioned by the Galactic Council," said Jessio. "I don't care about the children. I was just trying to blow General Foxwell into smithereens. Take the children's ship if you can. But get out of my way and leave me Foxwell."

"You put a virus in the justices. How was that helping them?" I asked.

"We suspected that the Heragi military had put in a second hidden prime directive in the justices. I just couldn't find it. If I could make the justices sick, then I would have time to review their code," explained Jessio.

"That little virus nearly killed them all," said Goggins.

"That's not what we meant to do," said Jessio. "But you've turned the Galactic Council against us."

"We didn't know, Jessio. You should have talked with the justices. Explained it to them," I said.

Stoller turned off the linked comm and came over just our inter-ship comm. "Gabe, I've got a clean shot at the towing line. I'm ready to take the shot on your command."

"Copy that, Stoller. I'll let Jeb know."

"No. Just notify Alex," said Stoller.

I thought about what he said. He was right. "Copy that."

I notified Alex of Stoller's plan and to be ready to accelerate.

"Okay, Stoller. On the count of three. One, two, three," I said.

Stoller fired a clean laser shot that clipped and severed the tow line. Alex punched it, and the *Ravena* cruised away from the *Firestone*.

Foxwell cursed and yelled at his crew. Then his comm stopped.

Jeb came over the line. "What the hell, Gabe?"

"Sorry," I yelled as Foxwell's *Firestone* opened fire on us and the *Otessis*. Then the *Sundra* fired on the *Firestone*. The *Ravena* was behind us, taking position to help fire upon the *Firestone*. Stoller was off firing back at the *Firestone*. This wasn't good. Too many ships firing, and I wasn't sure who Jessio was going to choose to fire upon.

"Alex, stay behind me. Don't get caught in this," I yelled in the comm to the *Ravena*.

"We're fine, Gabe. We want to help," said Alex. "Honora is piloting. I'm on the turret." The *Ravena* fired on the *Firestone*. I didn't like it one bit. The *Ravena* was a fine little ship, but one blast from the *Firestone* could seriously damage the *Ravena* due to its smaller size.

"Keep your eye on Jessio, too," I yelled at Stoller.

"Copy that."

"Gabe," said Jeb. "Jessio's ship. It's gone. It's got a cloaking system."

"Copy that." I should have anticipated this. Jessio had used the cloaking system on us when he was trying to retrieve the justices from us.

"Zara, can you hack into Jessio's ship and disable its cloaking system?" I asked.

"Already been on it since we saw him," she said as she worked hard on her coder, looking up to her monitor as code streamed by.

"Thank goodness," said Goggins.

We were hit hard by a missile from the *Sundra*. We all got thrown to the starboard side. "Feti, damage report," I yelled.

"He's on our port," yelled Stoller. "Turn her around."

I turned the *Alyssia* around as fast as I could to get Stoller in good shooting range. Jeb fired on the *Firestone* to give us some cover and then he shot in the area he thought the Sundra may be but those were misses. The *Sundra* then fired upon the *Ravena*. It was a direct hit. The *Ravena* was stunned. Its engines were out.

"They got the *Ravena*," yelled Goggins.

"Copy that," I said.

"This is not good, Gabe." Stoller continued to fire in the area he thought the *Sundra* was located but he was only guessing at this point.

"Zara?" I yelled.

"I need more time," Zara shouted back.

"Gabe, we have one engine failing," reported Feti.

"Shut it down, Feti. Balance power on our remaining engines," I responded. "Honora? Alex? What's going on?"

"We're okay. I mean the ship isn't, but we are, for the moment," said Honora.

"I'm sending out a line. We need to get it attached to you, and we'll tow you in," I said.

Goggins got up. "I'll help with the line." He ran to the hull.

"Feti, release a rescue line to the *Ravena*."

"Copy that, Gabe," said Feti.

We were hit hard again.

"Gabe, do you have the kids?" asked Jeb.

"Sending out a rescue line now."

"I'll go in hard to distract Foxwell," said Jeb as he raced in and fired upon the *Firestone*.

Goggins got on the comms. "That last hit got our tow line, Gabe. It's gone."

"Blasted," I said under my breath.

The *Ravena* drifted by us. They were helpless.

"Jeb, our tow rope is destroyed. Can you pick up the kids?" I asked. At that moment, Jeb was hit hard by the cloaked *Sundra*. He spun out of the firing area.

"Got it! Sundra's cloaking is down," yelled Zara.

Before our eyes, the *Sundra* appeared.

Then, out of nowhere, two missiles appeared and directly hit the *Sundra*. They blew apart two of its engines and knocked out its comm tower.

"Where the heck did that come from?" yelled Goggins as he ran onto the bridge.

An Oliverian naval destroyer ship appeared.

Stoller came over the comms. "It's Anjori!"

"I contacted the Oliverians when we were on our way to the Justice Station. Thank goodness they came," said Jeb.

Next the Oliverian ship took on *Firestone*. We could see the ship was already moving out, afraid of the power of the Oliverian ship.

"Look, there Foxwell goes," yelled Stoller.

The Oliverian shot out three missiles to keep General Foxwell running scared.

"Feti, get us a comm link with the Oliverian ship," said Jeb.

"Copy that," said Feti. "Go ahead."

"This is Jebediah Kell. Who do we have the pleasure of speaking with?"

"This is Colonel Bre," said a familiar voice.

And then a second voice also answered, "And General Anjori." A small Oliverian skiff docked next to the *Ravena*. "Picking up the Kell children to deliver them to the *Alyssia*."

"Copy that," I said.

"A two-fer," cackled Stoller as he came up to the bridge.

"See you soon," said Honora.

"Permission to dock, Gabe?" asked Jeb.

"The more the merrier," I said.

"Hey, that's something I would say," said Stoller.

"I hope he isn't rubbing off on you, Gabe," said Goggins.

"Would that be so bad?" I asked.

"Yes." Zara stared at me and then broke out in a smile.

Stoller, Goggins and I laughed. It felt good. We all pushed away from the *Sundra* that was sputtering in space. No one wanted to talk with Jessio. Further diplomacy could be worked on by Jebediah, but we had enough of Jessio for one sol.

We all greeted the Kell children, Alex, Honora and Talia, with hugs as we escorted them and Anjori to the galley. Jeb soon joined us, and we gathered around the galley table.

Alex had grown a bit since we were last together. Honora was smiling and sharing pilot stories with Stoller.

Talia had her real cicichimp, Cici, on her shoulder. She also held the robotic cicichimp that Goggins had given her. She sent me a thought. *Missed you.*

I missed you too.

Have you seen Synthia?

We picked her up from her home planet. We needed her help.

I want to see her.

We can arrange that. She's back on the Justice Station with your parents.

Jeb got up to say something. "Everyone, I want to say a formal thank you to Anjori and the Oliverians."

Stoller pretended he was sleeping and snored loudly. Everyone laughed. He pretended to wake up. "Sorry, I was just put to sleep."

Jeb shook his head at Stoller, who just smiled and pulled out a bottle of gin. "How about a real celebration?"

Goggins retrieved glasses, and the adults had a shot to raise. The kids got some goggleberry juice, and I raised an empty glass.

"To the Oliverians," started Stoller. "Their bravery is as big as their bones!" He raised his glass and everyone cheered. The seven-foot tall Anjori nodded and downed her shot. She stood up and towered over everyone.

"Thank you, Jebediah and Stoller. We're happy to help our friends. My sister, Swina, myself and Colonel Bre are very concerned about the Rothworths leaving the Galactic Council. We just got back from deep space, and we have news to share with you."

Feti interrupted our celebration. "Gabe? Sorry to interrupt. I have an urgent message."

"Go ahead, Feti," I said.

"There is something wrong back on the Justice Station. One of the justices is ill," it said. "That is all the message said. It was from Ava."

I glanced back at Goggins and Zara. They both were bewildered and shook their heads.

"Looks like the party is over, folks," said Stoller has he put the cap back on his bottle of gin.

"We'll follow you to the station," said Anjori. "We'll tow the *Ravena* back to the Justice Station."

"Thank you," said Honora.

"I'll lead the way," said Jeb as he also left for his ship.

"What could it be?" I asked Goggins and Zara. "The virus?"

"Not sure," said Zara.

"I hope not," said Goggins.

The bridge was silent for our return to the Justice Station. Everyone was concerned and had the worst expectation on their minds. It was hard to talk. We didn't know which justice was ill and if it was just a matter of time before the other justices would also succumb if it was the virus.

We followed Jeb and docked at the Justice Station within a few hours. Jeb exited to talk with the Galactic Council and give them an update.

The Galactic Council Police met us at our gate and escorted us out. The pedestrians bumped into us, but we kept going forward to the medbay on the first floor where Dr. Julipo had his lab.

We entered the medbay, and the lab was now being led by Ava and Damiel. All three justices lay on tables in the center of the room. They were wired to nearby monitors. The Kell children hugged their parents. Goggins and Zara went immediately to the monitors to begin understanding the situation and helping.

Jeb, Stoller and I stayed in the back of the room to give space for the medtech team to work. We felt helpless. There was nothing for a pilot to do. We could fight, shoot and fire missiles at fast moving enemy ships, but for right now, the scientists were in charge of this room and helping the Supreme Court justices.

After an hour, Ava and Damiel came over to us as we sat in chairs just watching them work.

"Thank you for bringing the children back here," said Ava.

"Of course," said Jeb. "What's wrong with the justices?"

"We thought only one was ill," said Stoller.

"Guy and Tefara," said Damiel.

"The virus came back," said Ava.

"Then why is Lilou also hooked up to monitors?" I asked.

"We are using her code, sort of like a vaccine," said Damiel. "Her code seems immune to the virus."

"We're just now trying to understand it," said Ava.

"Will they be okay?" asked Jeb. I knew what he was asking. He was politely trying to ask his brother and sister-in-law if there was a strong chance that Guy and Tefara could die.

"The virus is now throughout both their systems. The next few hours will tell us more," said Damiel.

"Is there anything we can do?" I asked.

"Pray. If you do that sort of thing," said Ava turning away.

19

———————

Stoller and I took a stroll out to the observatory deck at the Justice Station. We both needed to get out of the lab for a few moments. Seeing the ill justices and our team trying to save them was hard when you had no skill to help them.

We sat in two chairs looking out to the Edge.

"Tell me about what is out there," I asked.

Stoller's eyebrows rose on his face. "So much. I'd never have enough lifetimes to see it all." He chuckled. "But you would."

He was right. I would. Perhaps that was what intrigued me so much about the Edge.

"We would have to get a faster ship. Something that could jump light years with twice the velocity," he said.

I nodded. "Are they available?"

"Sure. Anything's available if you have enough money. Hard part is that Edward Gates' company is the one making those fast starships. And I don't think he's a fan of yours since you stole the *Alyssia* from him."

"His loss then," I said followed by a grunt-laugh.

"Maybe Zara is right and I am rubbing off on you," said Stoller with a wink.

"I'm in no danger of drinking too much gin, like you," I retorted.

"Yes, and that's why I like you even more. You don't drink my gin, and you can be my designated driver."

We both laughed.

I received a notice on my arm comm from one of the Kell children. "This is Gabe."

"Where are you?" asked Honora.

"Up on the observatory deck with Stoller."

"We're coming up," she said and ended the comm.

"The kids?" asked Stoller.

"Yes."

"I've missed them. What trouble have they been getting themselves into?"

"Finding Heragians like themselves," I answered.

"With the ancient gifts?"

"Yes," I said and pulled up my hand and held up a finger as I said each gift out loud, "Telekinesis like our Alex possesses, telepathy which Talia and even Honora share and spontaneous healing that Honora alone has mastered."

"That's amazing," said Stoller. "But I can't say I'm envious. With great power comes great responsibility. And I don't want too much of that."

I turned to him. "It's incredible what they possess."

"I agree," said Stoller.

"Imagine what they can do to help people," I said, and my thoughts wandered. What they could do…Honora could heal.

"Honora!" I shouted.

"Yes, she has that gift," he said, not understanding what I was trying to stress. "I remember when she healed my arm when we were fighting Kaleb Kron. My arm shredded right off, and look at it today. Not a scratch." He lifted his arm to examine it.

"She can *heal* the justices," I said.

Stoller popped up in his chair, curious about what I had just said.

Just then, the three Kell children arrived. Honora was leading her sister Talia up and Alex was following them. Stoller waved them over to our location.

"Found you," said Honora as she sat down next to us.

"Hey, we thought we'd keep you company," said Alex.

Talia's responder said, "We feel so bad about the justices."

"We've got to go back down to the lab. Now!" I said, getting up. "All of us."

"What? What's going on?" asked Honora.

"You can heal them," I said.

"With your gifts. Remember how you healed my arm?" said Stoller as he lifted up his arm.

Honora looked at us like we were crazy. "I can heal wounds. Bio matter. I've never healed a machine."

"I don't think that is how it works," said Talia's responder.

"We need to try," I said.

"Okay," said Honora as she turned to go to the lab. "I hope I can help."

We all rushed back down to the lab. I was feeling hopeful and actually felt a warmth in my chest. Honora talked with her parents. "Let me try," she said.

"But you can't heal code," said Damiel.

Ava rubbed her daughters' arm. "I don't think that is within your powers."

"Where is Synthia?" asked Talia's responder.

Sitting in the back of the room meditating was Synthia. She opened her eyes and stood. Talia ran up to her. They were sharing thoughts. I decided to join them.

Could it work? asked Talia in her mind.

It may, thought Synthia.

Mom and Dad believe it only works on organic materials.

We can only try, said Synthia as she approached Honora and her parents.

Lilou reached out her hand to me. I took it, and she pulled me close. She sent me a thought. *What is happening, Gabe? I was able to pick up a few of Talia's thoughts. Can her sister, Honora, heal them?*

We are going to try, I thought back.

Guy and Tefara were no longer responding and were lying on the gurneys with Zara and Goggins reviewing their code and consciousness levels closely. Goggins shook his head. His face was awash in worry.

We watched as Honora discussed a few items with Synthia. They inspected Guy and Tefara and then conferred more with Zara, Goggins, Ava and Damiel. Synthia then kissed Honora on the cheek. Honora sent me a thought. *I will try my best, Gabe.*

That is all I ask, I replied in a thought.

Honora first walked up to Guy. She put both of her hands over his head and closed her eyes. She stayed there and slowly moved down his body with her hands elevated just a few inches away from his armor. At times, she would touch him. We watched her circle him.

Honora then opened her eyes and moved over to Tefara and did the same ritual. I could tell that Honora was very tired by the time she circled Tefara. She opened her eyes halfway and then started to faint.

Damiel caught his daughter and laid her down on a nearby table. Ava ran over.

"Honora," Ava said as she wiped her daughter's hair from her eyes. Synthia came up and helped with Honora.

"I'm okay," said Honora, "Just very tired."

I crossed to Goggins and Zara. The justices' codes were streaming by on their monitors. "Did it work?"

Damiel also reviewed the code.

"I don't see any change," said Goggins.

"Neither do I," said Damiel as he stepped closer to the monitors.

"Honora's healings are instantaneous," I said.

"I'm afraid it didn't help," said Zara.

"Has Lilou attained the virus yet?" I asked.

Damiel reviewed the monitor with Lilou's code. "No, she hasn't."

"Not yet," said Goggins.

"What if she is immune?" I asked.

"How would that be? If she was never infected?" asked Zara.

"No, what if she was infected. The first time and even now, but her body fights the virus," I said as I began to think this all through.

"Do you mean she is somehow immune to the virus?" asked Ava, holding Honora, who was feeling better. Synthia also joined us with Stoller.

"Lilou is a Heragi," said Synthia.

"Yes," I said.

"She has the ancient gifts," continued Synthia.

"Lilou may have the gift of healing, too," I explained. "And maybe now, now that she is a robot, she can heal inorganic material."

Lilou got up from her table. "I heard what you said, Gabe."

"I don't know if it would work. But it's worth a try, isn't it?"

She nodded. "Of course. I want to try."

"Synthia, Honora. Please take Lilou and review what you can with her. We don't have the luxury of time," said Ava.

Synthia and Honora led Lilou into the corner to discuss the healing arts with her. Talia came up and slipped her hand into mine. I softly squeezed her hand.

I believe, was the thought that Talia sent me.

Yes, we needed to believe.

"Robots healing robots," said Goggins as he put his hands through his hair. I could tell his mind was being stretched now more than ever before.

"I wish Dr. Julipo could be here to witness this," said Zara as she sat down. Goggins put his hand on her shoulder.

"I think he's in a GC holding cell right now. So he isn't witnessing much besides the changing of the guards," said Goggins.

"He did the justices wrong, but I find no comfort in anyone being in a jail cell," said Stoller as he shook his head.

"He did the galaxy wrong," said Alex.

"True, but he has a lot to still offer the galaxy with all of his knowledge," said Goggins. "If only he hadn't wasted his gifts."

Lilou, with Honora and Synthia, came back to the center of the room.

"Are you ready?" asked Ava.

"Yes," said Lilou. "I believe so."

Talia squeezed my hand, and we all backed away to give Lilou room to heal her friends.

Lilou went to Guy and raised her hands. She lowered her head. Then reached down and her hand touched his head. She then lifted her hands and circled around his body as she held both hands out.

She then went to Tefara and held her hands over her.

Synthia and the Kell children had their eyes closed. They were in meditation to help and support Lilou. I closed my eyes.

I went into my mind and built the cube that Synthia had taught me. I pulled in Lilou's image.

She appeared in my mind. Her blue eyes were open, and her hands were out before her body.

They are so ill, Gabe, she thought to me.

I know. You can help them, Lilou.

Can I?

Yes.

Then Lilou disappeared from my cube. I opened my eyes. She had finished walking around Tefara's body. Lilou lowered her hand, and her gaze went to the ceiling.

Ava reached out to her. "Are you okay? Please sit."

She and Damiel escorted the justice to a nearby chair so she could rest.

We all went to the monitors that Goggins and Zara were staring at. Goggins scanned Guy's and Tefara's code.

"It's reducing. The virus is vanishing. Look!" Goggins backed away for others to see.

Damiel rushed up to the monitors. "The code is self-cleaning. She did it." He put his wife in front of the screen.

"I wouldn't have believed it," said Ava. "It worked. Their code is improving."

"Ha!" Zara high-fived Goggins.

Stoller came up from the back of the room. "She's got the gift. Lilou can heal." He turned to Zara, and they hugged.

Lilou came up to me and leaned against me. "You did it," I said. She put her head on my shoulder. I embraced her. The Kell children surrounded us and put their hands on her shoulders.

"Lilou, you saved Guy and Tefara," said Honora.

"Look, they're back online," said Goggins.

They were waking. Lilou went over to them and held their hands.

Stoller came up to me. "You were right, Gabe. Lilou had it in her."

"How did it work?" asked Zara.

"Robots curing robots?" asked Goggins. "I guess they won't need us anymore."

"It's because she does have a consciousness," said Ava. "Dr. Julipo and Dr. Redford were able to code it."

"And somehow she can cure her own kind, non-organic material, unlike Honora or other Heragians, I assume," said Damiel.

"Mother, does Gabe have a consciousness?" asked Alex.

Ava raised her eyebrows at me. "Gabe?"

"Let me answer," said Synthia as she stepped forward. "From my learnings with the ancient ones, all matter, including machines, have a consciousness. It may not be detectible or we can argue on the definition."

"Where does it come from?" asked Talia's responder.

"From their creators," said Synthia as she raised her hands up to Ava and Damiel and then pointed her hands back to me. "Gabe received his consciousness from small parts that came from Damiel and Ava."

"How does that work?" asked Honora.

"That is the mystery of our universe," said Synthia.

The justices were now all sitting up and talking. Lilou was informing the others of what happened. They all held hands.

"I'd like to make a motion. I move that we all discuss the mysteries of the universe at the Cup of Justice bar. How's that sound?" said Stoller.

"I second that motion," said Goggins.

"Those in favor?" asked Stoller.

"Aye," said Zara. Then the Kell children voiced their "Ayes."

"Of course, those underage can imbibe in goggleberry juice," said Stoller with a wink.

Ava, Damiel and I stayed with the justices and assisted them up to their apartments on the top floor of the Justice Station with a promise to later meet Stoller and everyone at the bar.

I wanted to be with the justices. Ava and Damiel left us alone after saying goodnight to all of us robots.

We sat in Lilou's apartment and dimmed the lights to look out to the spectacular view of the Edge.

Tefara grabbed a blanket off the couch and put it around her and Guy. She laughed. "I know I don't need this blanket. That my armor is self-regulated for hot and cool temperatures, but I want it around me. I want to feel its touch on my fingers. Does that make sense?"

Lilou leaned in and touched Tefara's knee. "Of course, it does."

"I like it too," said Guy as he tightened the blanket around him.

"It's the small things, isn't it?" said Lilou. "That may keep us sane."

"Yes, I believe so," I said. "And each other."

We leaned back into our seats watching the starships come and go from the Justice Station. We talked about the evening and how Lilou felt when she was healing Guy and Tefara. We talked like old friends. And it was nice. It was familiar.

I believed then, for the first time, that the justices were going to be okay. That they would grow together, not old, but grow together for a long, long time. After an hour, I decided to meet with my team down at the bar.

"Will you all be okay?" I asked.

"Yes," said Lilou. "Thank you, Gabe."

"You're welcome," I said. "I will see you all tomorrow."

"And then what? Will you be off on a mission?" asked Tefara.

"To deal with the Heragi Empire or Jessio?" asked Guy.

"I will need an update from Jebediah. That may be the case," I said.

"Will you visit us?" asked Lilou.

"Yes, I promise," I said.

"Good," she said.

I said goodbye and went down to the Cup of Justice bar. As I was taking the escalators down, I thought of what Synthia said about how creators give a part of their consciousness to what they are creating.

That would mean that a part of Dr. Julipo and Dr. Redford

were inside the justices. And part of Dr. Julipo was also inside Dr. Redford.

My mind was starting to fill up. I shook my head. That meant Ava and Damiel gave up a part of their consciousness to me. They were inside me.

My chest warmed.

I saw my team as I walked through the doors of the bar. The Kell children were drinking their juices and were warmly snuggled in with their parents, Ava and Damiel. Jeb had his arm resting on his brother's shoulder.

Stoller was holding court at the table. He was in his element as he was doing card tricks that had Goggins flustered as usual. Zara was shaking her head and skeptical of Stoller's tactics.

Synthia tilted her head back and laughed as her and Talia's cicichimps played at their feet.

I joined my team. It was a good sol to be a robot.

THE END

If you enjoyed this adventure, you can read more about Gabe and the team in HARMONIX, Book 4 in the Rogue Robot series.

AUTHOR NOTES

Dear Reader,

Thank you for reading Justice - Book 3 in the Rogue Robot Series! I hope you enjoyed the book.

I love writing about Gabe, our sentient robot. Over the past year I've planned out the series and learn more about Gabe and all the characters with each book that comes to fruition. I'm excited to show you where they all end up. Thanks again!

Want a little more? "HARMONIX" is Book 4 in the Rogue Robot series and is available to buy now! Continue reading the adventures with Gabe and his team as they take on the Heragi Empire.

Also, I've written a free bonus prequel novella e-book with Gabe, Ava, Damiel and Goggins called *Robots Don't Cry*. It takes place a few months before "Rogue" Book 1 starts. You can get this free prequel novella e-book, along with updates on new books in the series and future bonus materials by hitting this link and **signing up for my newsletter** on my website at **www. MegFoster.com.**

I've enjoyed spending time with Gabe and all the characters in the series. If you really liked the book and want to read more

Rogue Robot adventures, please consider leaving a review for Rogue and share the title with your friends. I'd appreciate it greatly!

Thank you!
 -Meg Foster

Books by Meg Foster

Rogue Robot Series:

ROBOTS DON'T CRY (prequel novella ebook)*
ROGUE (Book 1)
CYBS (Book 2)
JUSTICE (Book 3)
HARMONIX (Book 4)
TRINITY (Book 5)
CODA (Book 6)

*Only available when signing up for
Meg's newsletter.

This series is meant to be read in order.

About the Author

Sci-fi author **Meg Foster** explores the pitfalls and triumphs of human nature and technology. She reaches out to make us think and experience a wide range of emotions through her unique voice. Meg's meaningful and mirthful writing delivers stories we can savor and enjoy.

In addition to writing novels, Meg is a filmmaker and wrote, directed and produced the comedy/drama film "Stealing Roses" starring John Heard and Cindy Williams.

She was born in Detroit, Michigan and received a B.A. in Film Production from Southern Illinois University at Carbondale. When she isn't writing or enjoying the lakes and mountains near her home in the Pacific Northwest, you can find her online at www.MegFoster.com.

Also find Meg on Facebook where she has a private FB Group where readers come together, have fun, discuss the series, and speak directly with her at www.facebook.com/TheMegFoster.

Thank you for reading!

www.ingramcontent.com/pod-product-compliance
Lightning Source LLC
Chambersburg PA
CBHW030625190726
48286CB00008B/2396